Five to One

It only took Slocum a second to take in the sight in front of him. Coyote had his back to the farthest wall of the kitchen area and was holding Minh. It didn't take much imagination to figure out the intentions of the man with his pants down. A third armed man stood in the corner of the cabin where Minh kept her exotic supplies and mysterious jars. The fellow with the shotgun was closest to the door, and a fifth gunman was near the foot of Minh's bed.

Coyote kept his grip on Minh's neck and pulled her in front of him. "The money on this witch's scalp goes to us!" he said. "You want her, you'll have to fight for her!"

Smiling scornfully, Slocum replied, "That shouldn't be much of a problem . . ."

DON'T MISS THESE
ALL-ACTION WESTERN SERIES
FROM THE BERKLEY PUBLISHING GROUP

THE GUNSMITH by J. R. Roberts
Clint Adams was a legend among lawmen, outlaws, and ladies. They called him . . . the Gunsmith.

LONGARM by Tabor Evans
The popular long-running series about Deputy U.S. Marshal Custis Long—his life, his loves, his fight for justice.

SLOCUM by Jake Logan
Today's longest-running action Western. John Slocum rides a deadly trail of hot blood and cold steel.

BUSHWHACKERS by B. J. Lanagan
An action-packed series by the creators of Longarm! The rousing adventures of the most brutal gang of cutthroats ever assembled—Quantrill's Raiders.

DIAMONDBACK by Guy Brewer
Dex Yancey is Diamondback, a Southern gentleman turned con man when his brother cheats him out of the family fortune. Ladies love him. Gamblers hate him. But nobody pulls one over on Dex . . .

WILDGUN by Jack Hanson
The blazing adventures of mountain man Will Barlow—from the creators of Longarm!

TEXAS TRACKER by Tom Calhoun
J. T. Law: the most relentless—and dangerous—manhunter in all Texas. Where sheriffs and posses fail, he's the best man to bring in the most vicious outlaws—for a price.

JAKE LOGAN

SLOCUM
AND
THE WITCH OF
WESTLAKE

J
JOVE BOOKS, NEW YORK

THE BERKLEY PUBLISHING GROUP
Published by the Penguin Group
Penguin Group (USA) Inc.
375 Hudson Street, New York, New York 10014, USA
Penguin Group (Canada), 90 Eglinton Avenue East, Suite 700, Toronto, Ontario M4P 2Y3, Canada
(a division of Pearson Penguin Canada Inc.)
Penguin Books Ltd., 80 Strand, London WC2R 0RL, England
Penguin Group Ireland, 25 St. Stephen's Green, Dublin 2, Ireland (a division of Penguin Books Ltd.)
Penguin Group (Australia), 250 Camberwell Road, Camberwell, Victoria 3124, Australia
(a division of Pearson Australia Group Pty. Ltd.)
Penguin Books India Pvt. Ltd., 11 Community Centre, Panchsheel Park, New Delhi—110 017, India
Penguin Group (NZ), 67 Apollo Drive, Rosedale, North Shore 0632, New Zealand
(a division of Pearson New Zealand Ltd.)
Penguin Books (South Africa) (Pty.) Ltd., 24 Sturdee Avenue, Rosebank, Johannesburg 2196,
South Africa

Penguin Books Ltd., Registered Offices: 80 Strand, London WC2R 0RL, England

SLOCUM AND THE WITCH OF WESTLAKE

A Jove Book / published by arrangement with the author

PRINTING HISTORY
Jove edition / April 2009

ISBN: 978-0-515-14606-6

JOVE®
Jove Books are published by The Berkley Publishing Group,
a division of Penguin Group (USA) Inc.,
375 Hudson Street, New York, New York 10014.
JOVE is a registered trademark of Penguin Group (USA) Inc.
The "J" design is a trademark of Penguin Group (USA) Inc.

PRINTED IN THE UNITED STATES OF AMERICA

10   9   8   7   6   5   4   3   2   1

1

A shot cracked through the air, sending a chunk of lead toward John Slocum's head. Since he was peeking out from behind a rock, all Slocum had to do was pull his head back and pray his reflexes were fast enough to save his life. The bullet sparked against the side of the rock, sending a jagged piece of the boulder flying amid a shower of sparks.

Slocum gritted his teeth and leaned out from the other side of the boulder to send a few shots of his own toward the owlhoots that were trying to drill holes through him. He squeezed the trigger of his Colt Navy until his ears were filled with thunder and the acrid taste of burnt gunpowder coated the back of his throat.

Even though he knew he hadn't hit much of anything, Slocum did hear the sounds of boots scraping against the sunbaked dirt.

"Missed us, asshole!" one of the gunmen in the distance shouted. "And you're about to be surrounded!"

Slocum grinned and shook his head as he reloaded his pistol. There were at least three men shooting at him. They'd ambushed him from a good spot along a stretch of trail bordered by a ridge on one side and a rushing river on the other. While the bushwhackers had succeeded in planning, however, they were falling short in execution, relying on numbers and constant gunfire instead of trying to place a few good hits.

Then again, since Slocum was the one hiding behind a rock that looked more like a tombstone, he figured it was a bit early to chalk this fight up as a victory.

Picturing the terrain in his head, Slocum held his six-shooter at the ready and pushed away from the boulder on the side that had recently been chipped. The only gunman he saw couldn't have been out of his late teens. The kid held a gun in each hand, but looked too rattled to use them effectively.

Slocum took advantage of the kid's inexperience and charged straight for him like a crazed bull. Although the kid pulled himself together fairly quickly, it wasn't quick enough. Slocum was already in striking distance and wasn't about to waste his chance.

From such close range, all Slocum had to do was aim from the hip and squeeze off a shot. The Colt Navy barked once and tore a piece of meat from the kid's thigh. It was a messy hit, but more than enough to send the kid down amid a spray of blood and a flurry of obscenities.

"You're dead, you son of a—" was all the kid got out before the handle of Slocum's gun silenced him. The polished wooden grip cracked against the kid's jaw and snapped his head to one side.

"Yeah, yeah," Slocum grunted as he dropped to one knee beside the wounded kid. "Save the tough talk for your friends. Speaking of them, where'd they go?"

"Probably lining up a shot right now," the kid replied as he realized he hadn't dropped his pistol. His hand was shaking, but he brought the gun up a few inches before Slocum dropped his own pistol like an ax, smashing the kid's hand into the dirt. When the kid looked up again, he was staring straight down the barrel of Slocum's Colt. "Don't shoot, Brady! He'll kill me!"

The firing from the other gunmen stopped just long enough for one angry voice to cut through the air. "Kill him first then!" it said.

Slocum chuckled and looked toward the sound of that voice. "Doesn't sound like you boys are too friendly."

The kid at Slocum's feet was so mad, he barely noticed when Slocum kicked one of his twin pistols away and grabbed the other for himself. "I been trying to kill the prick!" the kid shouted. "What the hell else would I be doing?"

There were a few saplings surrounded by some shrubs nearby, so Slocum dragged the kid behind them. It wasn't the best cover he could think of, but it was the closest. Apart from those shrubs and the tombstone boulder, there was a wide clearing filled with a few more trees scattered about. The river was to Slocum's back at the moment. He'd been filling his canteen there when the three young gunmen had so rudely introduced themselves. They'd come at him in a hurry amid a storm of gunfire. After that, it was all Slocum could do to keep from catching any of those bullets.

Suddenly, Slocum felt his luck take a turn for the better. "Ah," he said as he fixed his eyes upon a pair of horses standing on the other side of the river. "I see you're just the fellas I've been looking for. Glad to see you brought those horses."

"What horses?" the kid on the ground asked.

"The horses that should be grazing on the Singer spread right now instead of standing on the other side of that river."

The kid actually twisted on his back to look toward the water's edge. "Oh, them horses? We found those."

Another shot cracked through the air, but it didn't come from a pistol. Slocum recognized the report of a Winchester when he heard it, and he guessed the one that had just been fired was no more than fifty or sixty yards away. Although the rifle's bullet hadn't hit him, Slocum dropped onto his belly before the man behind that Winchester got lucky.

The kid on the ground was still squirming from the fresh wound in his thigh. Keeping his hand pressed against the bloody flesh, the kid started crawling away from the bushes. Slocum grabbed the kid by the shirt and hauled him back as if he was dragging a stray pup by the scruff of its neck.

"The Singers want their horses back," Slocum growled. "They'll also pay for your hides. If your friends get away with them animals, I'll just have to drag you back to answer for all your partners. Let's just say there's a bonus in it for me if you're in bad enough shape to bring a smile to the Singers' faces."

Judging by the panicked look on the kid's face, he didn't like the sound of that one bit.

Slocum slammed the kid down so his shoulders hit the ground with enough force to take the wind from his lungs. "Keep those other two from leaving, and I might see my way clear to just take the horses," Slocum said.

After thinking it over for all of two seconds, the kid hollered, "Come on over here! I got him!"

A few silent moments passed before Brady shouted back, "Where is he?"

"Right here, dammit!"

"Stand up so we can see you."

Despite the fact that Brady wasn't buying the kid's claim, Slocum had heard enough to narrow down Brady's location to within a few yards. That way, when he bolted from behind the shrubs, Slocum had a good idea of where to direct his fire.

Slocum kept his head down as he rushed around the bushes. Knowing his first shots would be wild, he fired them from the pistol he'd taken from the kid. Those shots flushed Brady out from behind the tree he'd been using for cover and sent the man running toward the river.

The moment Slocum heard the hammer of the kid's gun

slap against the back of an empty casing, he tossed the pistol away and brought up his Colt Navy. He fired one shot at Brady, which clipped the man's shoulder and sent Brady staggering to one side. Before he could fire another shot, Slocum heard the distinctive bark of the Winchester behind him. He reflexively launched himself to the right as the rifle's bullet hissed past him.

Slocum hit the ground on his side, rolled toward the river, and fired a shot at Brady. His bullet sent the man into the water, but Slocum wasn't about to sit still long enough to find out any more than that. Instead, he got back up on one knee, steadied his aim, and fired toward the puff of smoke hanging in the air to mark the spot where the Winchester had been fired.

It was too much to hope that the shot had drawn blood, but Slocum did see a figure leap from behind a tree toward one of the smaller rocks jutting from the ground. Slocum flipped open his Colt and replaced the empty bullet casings with fresh rounds from his gun belt. By the time he was through reloading, he was back on his feet and running for cover behind the same tree Brady had abandoned.

The moment Slocum's shoulder bumped against the sturdy trunk, another round from the Winchester punched through the tree a few inches from his face. Wood chips sprayed through the air and spattered against Slocum's cheek. That round was followed by another, which tore away more of the weathered bark.

"Damn it," Slocum growled as he hunkered down and looked for another source of cover. Every shot from that Winchester chipped away at the tree he was using, while also drawing closer to Slocum's hide in the process. Another few shots and the rifleman would find his mark.

Since his cover was quickly losing its value and the other two gunmen were surely circling to get a better angle, Slocum knew that waiting in his spot was no longer an option. He snatched his hat from his head and tossed it away. As soon as he heard the Winchester fire at the movement, Slocum ran in the opposite direction.

As he moved, he did his best to judge where the rifleman was firing from. After a few rushed steps, Slocum was able to get a look at the back side of the rock the rifleman had ducked behind and fire a quick shot at him.

The rifleman nearly jumped out of his skin when the sparks flew from the rock directly in front of him. By the time he turned toward Slocum, another shot was headed his way. This one hissed past him like an angry hornet and caused his finger to twitch against his trigger.

Slocum planted his feet and extended his arm so he could sight along the top of his Colt's barrel. "Drop it!" he shouted.

But the rifleman didn't take Slocum's advice. Instead, he lifted the Winchester to his shoulder so he could take another shot. At least, he tried to lift the Winchester before Slocum stopped him dead in his tracks.

The Colt Navy spat its lead with a fiery roar and dropped the rifleman to the dirt. Slocum rushed over to where the rifleman had fallen before he tried to crawl away and join his friends. When he got close enough to see the rifleman's face, Slocum knew the man wasn't about to crawl anywhere. A bloody third eye had been drilled through his forehead. Even so, Slocum reached down to pick up the fallen man's weapon.

The Winchester was empty.

"Damn fool," Slocum muttered.

Hefting the rifle over his shoulder, Slocum hurried back to check on the other two gunmen. Brady was lying on his side on the riverbank. A messy hole had been torn through his side, which he favored by keeping it up and off the ground. Plenty of blood had seeped from the wound to mix with the dirt or be soaked into the man's clothes. Apparently, most of Brady's will to fight had drained out right along with it.

"Stay put," Slocum said, even though Brady was obviously too tuckered out to go anywhere. Slocum didn't have to look far to find the kid. The young fellow was dragging himself across the river toward the waiting horses. At the moment, the water was splashing up over his nose and occasionally washing over his head.

Slocum waded into the river, making certain to brush his feet against the bottom to keep from falling into any holes or stepping off any submerged ledges. Although rough and jagged, the bottom of the river seemed solid enough. Slocum got to the kid with only a few stumbles along the way. Despite the sogginess of his feet and the cold water seeping into his boots, Slocum couldn't help but laugh when he got to the kid's side.

"Where are you headed, boy?" Slocum asked.

The kid clawed another couple of inches, which only forced him to strain even harder to keep his head above water. Glancing over his shoulder, the kid grunted and continued to pull himself along.

Slocum took another step to keep up with him. "That wound's gotta be hurting an awful lot by now."

"I don't even feel it no more," the kid replied through gritted teeth.

"That ain't exactly a good thing."

"What the hell do you care?"

"I don't," Slocum said.

"Then let me get to the other side so I can . . . so I can fight you face-to-face!"

Slocum looked at the shore and then back down at the kid. "It looks a little farther than you can crawl, if you ask me."

"That shows what you know," the kid said. His voice was starting to tremble and his words were becoming more strained with every passing second. Even so, he looked up at Slocum and growled, "If you're too yellow to let me get to the other side . . . then you can go fu—"

Before the kid could finish his threat, Slocum grabbed a handful of his hair and shoved the kid's face down into the water. A few seconds later, Slocum pulled the kid up again and asked, "You want to keep talking tough or would you like to live a while longer?"

"I'd like to cut your—"

Slocum dunked the kid again and held his head under for a few seconds longer. It wasn't long enough to end the kid's thrashing, but it gave Slocum a chance to take another look back to find Brady still lying on his side, struggling to reach something in his boot.

Pulling the kid's head up again, Slocum said, "I'd pick my next words a bit more carefully if I were you."

The kid sputtered and coughed up some water, but was quickly losing steam. Finally, he nodded as best he could considering the grip Slocum had on the back of his head.

"That's more like it," Slocum said. Letting go of the kid's hair, he reached down to pull the kid back up to his feet.

As soon as the kid emerged from the water, he let out an agonized groan. The river wasn't too deep at that spot, but Slocum was just able to see the wound on the kid's thigh. Blood still ran from it, but it was being thinned by the water that poured down every inch of the young man's body.

Slocum draped one of the kid's arms over his shoulders and hoisted him from the water. When he felt the young man dragging his feet, Slocum said, "Maybe I should just let you drown. Is that what you're after?"

Grudgingly, the kid started to cooperate. As much as he wanted to walk on his own, the kid's wound was preventing him from doing much without Slocum's help. Running was out of the question and fighting was a pipe dream.

Once he'd dragged the kid to the riverbank, Slocum let the young man fall. After losing so much blood and gulping down so much river water, the kid couldn't keep himself from collapsing into a heap next to Brady.

"All right," Slocum said as he drew his pistol and aimed

it at Brady. "You want to toss that derringer away or should I just dump you into that river?"

Brady was a good-sized fellow with a burly frame and a scarred face. His hair was closely cropped for the most part, but jutted from his scalp at odd angles. He scowled up at Slocum with his arm still stretched down toward his left boot. Bony fingers were still wrapped around the little pistol that had been hidden there.

"Did you steal that gun from a lady?" Slocum asked.

Tossing the derringer into the river, Brady grunted, "Go to hell."

"I'm guessing you've got some more weapons stashed somewhere, so why don't you toss those as well?"

"Kiss my ass."

Slocum responded to that by leaning forward to smash his fist into Brady's jaw. The punch came quick enough to catch the man off his guard, and had more than enough wallop behind it to dim the fire in his eyes. Brady flopped onto his back and fell into an uncomfortable sleep.

"What about you?" Slocum asked as he shifted his eyes to the kid.

The youngest of the gunmen looked at Brady, and then glanced toward where the rifleman's corpse was lying in the grass. After that, he took a knife from one boot and threw it toward the water. Keeping his hand on his other boot, he grumbled, "The other one must'a already fell in when I was crawling."

Slocum could see the empty scabbard on that boot, so he nodded. "All right then. Tell me where the rest of the Singers' animals are."

"The horses are all over there," he replied. "You can see 'em from here!"

"What about the cows?"

"What cows?"

Slocum narrowed his eyes and extended his arm until the barrel of his Colt was about to tap against the kid's teeth.

"The Singer family is missing a dozen head of cattle from their herd, along with those horses over there. Since they're the ones putting up the money for the return of those animals, there's no reason for them to lie about them being missing."

"Maybe they're piss-poor ranchers and the cows wandered off," the kid shot back. "You ever think of that?"

"No," Slocum said. "Since I've been working on that ranch for the better part of a month, I didn't think along those lines." Thumbing back the pistol's hammer, he added, "Tell me where those cattle are or I'll just have to look for them on my own."

"We sold 'em off already," the kid quickly replied. "The man who bought 'em works some spread a few miles from here."

"What about the horses?" Slocum asked. "What were you planning on doing with them?"

"We were gonna sell them off in Westlake. Brady thought it would be too suspicious for us to try to unload 'em all at the same place. Besides, that rancher didn't look to have much money left."

"I'll bet you saw to that, didn't you?"

Suddenly, the defiance had completely disappeared from the kid's face. In its place was stark fear bordering on desperation. "We didn't rob him! We just sold him the cows!"

"What was the man's name?"

"Landry! He said his name was Landry, but we didn't ask for anything but the money, I swear!"

Slocum glared at the kid until sweat broke out from the young man's forehead to trickle down his face along with the river water. Once Slocum knew he wasn't going to get any more trouble from the gunman, he said, "There now. That wasn't so hard, was it?"

2

That night, Slocum rode across the property line of the Singer Moon Ranch. The spread was marked by the brand that was burned into the flanks of the remaining cattle wandering among the bits of grass that sprouted here and there. Knowing the name of the place made it easier to figure the meaning behind the big circle around the smaller circle and line that was as close to a musical note as an iron could get. Trailing behind Slocum were the horses he'd retrieved from Brady and the other two gunmen. Draped across the backs of three of their own horses were the gunmen themselves.

The sun was dipping below the western horizon, which meant the last rays of the day were cast directly into Slocum's face. Because of that, he didn't spot the approaching riders until they were close enough to shout at him.

"This is private property, mister," one of the riders said.

Shading his face with his hand, Slocum replied, "I know. I'm the one who painted the sign."

The rider who'd done the talking was Robbie. Slocum knew that much from the sound of the young man's voice. Robbie might have only been fresh out of his teens, but he'd already gotten enough credibility behind his name to have one of the highest spots among the Singer Moon ranch hands. Robbie leaned forward in his saddle and asked, "That you, John?"

"Yep," Slocum replied as he pulled down the bandanna that had been keeping his lungs from filling with trail dust.

"Who's that with you?"

"Those men that stole Hal's stock. One's got to be buried, but I figured Hal would want the whole lot of them."

After letting out a slow whistle, Robbie said, "The old man'll be happy to know you found those thieves. Why don't you take them to the barn until we figure out what to do with 'em?"

Slocum led the horses down a trail that cut straight through the middle of the ranch. As he drew closer to Robbie and the other ranch hand, Slocum heard the question he'd been waiting for the whole time.

"What about the cattle?" Robbie asked. "I don't suppose you found them somewhere along the way as well?"

"I found 'em all right," Slocum replied. "I just got hungry before getting all the way back here."

For a second, Robbie didn't know what to make of that. He craned his neck to try and get a better look at the trail stretching out behind Slocum and the other horses. He then shook his head and chuckled. "You didn't find any cattle," he grumbled.

Slocum smirked and patted Robbie's shoulder as he rode past. "You're too gullible. Stay away from the poker tables."

If Robbie had any more questions, he was too busy getting laughed at by the second ranch hand to ask them. As always, Robbie took the joshing well, and started firing some back before too long. Slocum kept his reins taut so he could watch the horses he was leading every step of the way. The two surviving gunmen were wrapped up too tightly to do much more than squirm, and the sight of their dead partner on the other horse's back did plenty to sap their will to fight.

The Singer Moon Ranch was a fairly impressive spread situated in the western portion of the Arizona Territory. Compared to some of the places Slocum had worked in Texas, it wasn't much more than a field, but the Singer family didn't have need for the sprawling property of a cattle baron. Their spread served their needs just fine, considering the modest size of their herd. For that reason, Hal Singer was mad enough to spit when his herd had been trimmed by rustlers.

It hadn't been Slocum's intention to spend as much time as he had at the ranch. He'd simply been riding west and found himself short on funds. As luck would have it, Hal Singer stumbled into the same saloon where Slocum was nursing a bottle of whiskey, and complained about his labor troubles loud enough to be heard by everyone in the place. Slocum needed money, and the prospect of sleeping in a real bed after a home-cooked meal was too good to pass up. Every time Slocum had collected his things to move on, Hal had bumped up his wages. Also, Hal's niece Kelly had some wiles of her own.

"What should we do with them rustlers?" Robbie asked once they'd ridden long enough to catch sight of the bunkhouse and family home built at the center of the property.

Slocum shrugged. "Pile 'em up with the hay bales for all I care."

Robbie winced. "Or I could keep them in the stables where some of the boys can keep an eye on them."

"Suit yourself."

Once he'd taken the reins from Slocum, Robbie led the reclaimed horses to the northern side of the ranch where a barn and large stable had been constructed.

"Make sure you watch them closely," Slocum warned. "And don't loosen those ropes!"

In the time Slocum had been there, he'd earned enough respect from the ranch hands for his orders to be taken seriously. Since he'd left the spread on his own and returned with the cattle rustlers in his custody, that respect seemed to have gone up a notch or two.

The closer he got to the houses, the more the other hands took notice of Slocum's return. By the time Robbie and his partner arrived at the stable, every available hand had gathered around to get a look at what Slocum had brought back. Since most of those hands were armed after the cattle had gone missing, Slocum wasn't too worried about them being able to watch a pair of wounded thieves trussed up like calves at a rodeo.

The hands weren't the only ones at the ranch to notice that Slocum had returned. Hal and Kelly Singer both stood on the porch of the family home, watching Slocum expectantly. Kelly was a tall redhead with generous curves and pale skin. She jumped excitedly and picked up her skirts so she could hop down from the porch and run to greet Slocum. Hal Singer stood an inch or two shorter than his niece and had a permanent scowl etched into his face. His mouth looked more like a crack in a rock face that had formed around one of the cheroots that had been clenched between his teeth since he and Slocum had first met.

Hal's cheroot was still in place, but it waggled a bit as a smirk made a rare appearance on his face. "By God, Slocum. Are those fellas you handed over who I think they are?"

"I would hope so," Slocum replied. "I'm not in the habit of tying up just anyone and dragging them along with me."

"Is that all of them?"

"I'm pretty sure of it. They don't strike me as the sort who would go through such lengths to let someone else get away."

Turning on his heels, Hal stomped toward the front door and motioned for Slocum to follow him. "Come on inside then. We've got some business to conduct."

Slocum swung down from his saddle and flipped his horse's reins around the post a few paces away from the porch. Kelly Singer had rushed up to him, and watched him intently with her hands clasped behind her back. Although she'd remained quiet until now, the effort of staying that way looked to be more than she could handle.

"I knew you'd find them," she said in a voice that tried to be a whisper, but had a little too much anxiety behind it.

Leaning toward her and matching her whisper, Slocum replied, "So did I."

"I've been waiting for you to get back."

"It's only been a day or two."

"Feels like longer."

Just then, the curtains covering the front window were pulled aside to let a woman peek through. Slocum could only see a portion of a wrinkled face, which didn't do much to narrow down the list of who might be checking on him. There were plenty of aunts, grandmothers, and workers who fit that description, and every last one of them was anxious to have something other than cows to watch.

Kelly must have felt those eyes on her, because she shot a quick glance over her shoulder toward the window. Whoever was peeking outside reacted to the glance as if it stung, and the curtains were quickly pulled back into place. "I'll make sure you get your favorite supper tonight," Kelly promised.

"What about dessert?"

There was just enough of a growl in Slocum's question to flush Kelly's cheeks. She chewed on her lower lip and nodded. "That, too," she said.

"Riding out on the trail by yourself can do things to a man," Slocum continued. "Makes him wild like all the animals out there."

In his time working for the Singers, Slocum had quickly learned how to get Kelly going. She was the sort of woman who was accustomed to fending off the clumsy advances of ranch hands, but wasn't quite used to being handled by someone with more experience. That, however, didn't mean she wasn't willing to learn, and Slocum had been doing his best to broaden her horizons.

Kelly lowered her head and averted her eyes. Even though she was tall for a woman, she suddenly seemed much smaller as she turned away and ran toward the house. Slocum gave her a few seconds before stepping inside himself. The house was well maintained and reflected the tastes of every last woman who lived there. To that end, Slocum felt like he was stepping into a shop that sold frilly doilies and porcelain statues. Possibly for that reason, Hal rarely invited his ranch hands into the house. When he did, the visit took place in the only room that wasn't decorated with lace or fringe.

Hal Singer's office was all sharp edges and animal pelts. Hunting trophies lined the walls, along with a collection of military sabers and bowie knives. A full bearskin rug covered a good section of the floor that wasn't taken up by the desk, which must have cost the lives of half a dozen oak trees.

"Have a seat, Slocum," Hal said from his perch on the edge of his desk. Stretching one toe down to touch the floor, the old man let his other foot dangle as he struck a match and touched the flame to his cheroot.

Slocum dropped himself into the chair positioned in front of the desk. He knew the old man preferred to look down on his employees, but Slocum was too tired to refuse the offer.

"Looks like you've been busy," Hal said.

Slocum removed his black hat so he could run a hand over the rumpled mess of hair beneath it. Letting out a sigh, he admitted, "Not as busy as it may look. Those three came to me before I found them."

"Why on earth would they do that?"

"I was filling my canteen when they ambushed me," Slocum told him. "I guess they wanted my horse, or perhaps they thought I was carrying a few dollars in my pockets."

"Or maybe they recognized you as one of my regulators," Hal pointed out.

Slocum chuckled and put his hat back on. "I'd say the smart money is on them wanting my horse. Besides, Hal, I'm not one of your regulators."

"The job's still open, you know. And the wages are more'n what any ranch hand will ever see."

"I'm sure they are, but this was a one-time job. I don't appreciate a bunch of cowardly rustlers sneaking in and helping themselves when I'm the one patrolling the fence for the night."

"Don't want to look bad, huh?" Hal asked as he gnawed on his cheroot. "No need to worry about that, my friend. Any man can get robbed when his back's turned, but not any man would ride out on his own to set things right again. For that, you earn high marks with me. High marks indeed."

Although the cattle had been stolen on the night when Slocum was supposed to be patrolling the fence line, things hadn't happened quite as folks thought. In fact, Brady and the other rustlers had simply chosen to sneak onto the Singer ranch while Slocum was tussling with Kelly under a blanket in the carriage house. No matter how good a tussle that had been, Slocum didn't think he would get such high marks from Kelly's uncle if he knew exactly how the rustlers had gotten onto the property. Hal had made one very good point, though. Slocum didn't like being made to look bad.

Perhaps it came from his upbringing or just from his own sense of pride, but Slocum couldn't bear to let some sneaky bastards waltz in under his nose and steal whatever they pleased. Whether he'd been guarding cattle, diamonds, or clay bricks, Slocum wasn't about to be slighted by the likes of Brady and those other two. Besides, Hal was offering more than enough of a reward to make it worth Slocum's while to rectify his mistake.

"Speaking of setting things right," Hal continued, "I

saw the horses being led back to the stable, but no cattle. Were they left out on the property to graze with the rest?"

"They're probably out grazing," Slocum admitted, "but not here."

The look in Hal's eyes might have been enough to rattle the younger men in his employ, but it didn't do much to Slocum. It conveyed what the old man thought about Slocum's comment, which was something much less than favorable. "This ain't funny to me, John. My herd is my livelihood."

Slocum nodded and leaned forward. Although he'd seen a lot worse than the angry fire in the older man's eyes, he appreciated where that fire had come from. "I know it's not funny, Hal. I didn't mean to make light of it."

"Then stop fooling about and tell me where the hell my cattle are! If those are the men that stole them, they should know."

"They do know," Slocum replied. "More than that, they told me."

"Go on."

"The said they sold the cattle to a man named Landry."

Suddenly, the fire in Hal's eyes was stoked to a full blaze. "As in the Landry who owns the spread bordering mine?"

"That's the first one that came to my mind," Slocum replied. "I don't know for certain if the brands were tampered with, but he had to know they were stolen."

"He had to know they were mine," Hal grunted as he slid off the edge of his desk and stormed around to sit in the large chair behind it. "That son of a bitch has been trying to chip away at my property line for years. He even tore down one of my fences and put it up again ten yards in his favor. Can you believe the gall? Like I wouldn't notice!"

Slocum did his level best to try to look concerned with Hal's grousing, but it wasn't easy. After he had listened to the old man squawk about his neighbors every chance he got, the tirades became just another rattle in the wind. "I intend on heading over to pay Landry a visit myself," Slocum said. "I was going to go there today, but it's getting dark and I figured I should stow those rustlers someplace safe before anything else."

"That's fine, but I expect you to go there come first light."

"That's what I intended on doing, Hal."

"And take one of my hands with you. Come to think of it, you should probably take two or three."

Reaching the end of his patience, Slocum stood up and asked, "Why don't I just take all of them? I know, let's just start a war with Landry. The two of you can shout and cuss at each other from the backs of your horses while your hired hands fire shots at each other with hunting rifles. That sounds like a real hoot!"

For a moment, Hal just gaped at Slocum from behind his desk. His mouth hung open just enough for his cheroot to droop. Before it fell completely from between his teeth, Hal took a puff from it and let out a smoky guffaw. "If any of my regulators talked to me like that, I'd have their head on a pike."

"You don't have regulators, Hal," Slocum pointed out. "You've got honest ranch hands that break their backs for you. This is a peaceful operation and there's no reason for that to change."

Hal nodded and rolled his cheroot between thumb and forefinger. "That's what I like about you, Slocum. You're a straight talker."

"Here's some more talk you should hear. You lost a few head of cattle, but we'll get them back. No need for any more blood to be spilled. Landry seems like the sort of man who doesn't want to start trouble. At least, not directly and not the sort of trouble that costs lives."

"You haven't been here long enough to know any better," Hal grunted. "He's a slimy rat who'll try to get a dollar any way he can. You'd know as much if you dealt with him like I have."

"Then I'll find out when I deal with him. Tomorrow." Slocum spoke that last word with his eyes fixed upon Hal Singer.

Slowly, Hal nodded. "I can wait till tomorrow, just as long as you guarantee Landry will get what's coming to him."

"What are you asking, Hal?"

The older man ground his teeth together as he contemplated the lit end of his cheroot. "Horse thieves are hung. Cattle rustlers deserve the same."

"I'm going there to get your property back," Slocum said. "Not to settle a dispute with a neighbor with a bullet."

"I'd pay you more for your trouble."

Slocum turned his back on the desk and headed for the door. "This conversation's over."

Jumping up from his chair, Hal raced around his desk to get to Slocum before he left the office. It was the fastest the rancher had moved in the short time Slocum had known him. "I ain't condoning murder, Slocum, you know that," Hal sputtered. "I'm just angry about what happened."

"Yeah, I can see that much."

"I guess I just thought, since it looks like you already killed one of those thieves already . . ."

"I shot that man before he shot me," Slocum pointed out. "There's a difference."

Hal nodded quickly and said, "Sure, sure. I've joked about putting Landry outta my misery and that's all this was. A joke."

"Fine, Hal. Real funny. I'm hungry and tired, so I hope this is the end of this conversation."

"Not hardly!" Once he saw the change in Slocum's expression, Hal grinned and added, "I owe you some money for bringing in those rustlers."

"You sure do. I'll take that along with my wages for the week."

Scowling as if he'd just been asked to hand over his first-born, Hal asked, "You want wages on top of the pay for riding out after them rustlers? That'd be gettin' paid for two jobs at once!"

"That's right. I did the job on my own after tending to the rest of the herd and painting that new sign."

Hal nodded and patted Slocum's shoulder. "True enough. But," he said as he used his cheroot to point at Slocum, "if those cattle aren't returned to me, I'll expect you to make up the cost of the fence that was broke when those cattle were stolen, and the money I'll lose if any of them animals were damaged or killed between here and the Landry place. They were stolen on your watch, after all."

As much as Slocum wanted to argue that point, he simply couldn't. On the other hand, that didn't make it any easier to let the rancher speak to him like he was a misbehaving child. "Tell you what," Slocum finally said. "I'll make it up to you by running another errand for you without pay."

Hearing that was enough to raise the rancher's eyebrows. "I'm listening."

"Those rustlers may not be too bright, but this couldn't have been their first job. That means there's probably some kind of price on their heads. I'll see to it they get ridden out to Sheriff Bilson and if there's a reward coming, I'll split it with you."

"I only get half?"

"Considering I did all the work in bringing them in, I'd say that's enough to make up for your inconvenience as well as any losses."

The smile that spread across Hal's face would have looked just as natural on a barracuda. "Depends on the bounty, but I'd say that sounds good." And just as quickly as it had appeared, the smile faded. "What if there ain't no bounty?"

"Then you can keep my wages for this last week."

Considering how much the rancher paid, that was a loss

Slocum could deal with. The reward Hal had offered for the capture of the rustlers was more than enough to make up for it.

Hal extended his hand. "It's a deal, Slocum."

"Good to hear it," Slocum replied while shaking the hand that had been offered. "Now I'm going to see if there's any stew left in the bunkhouse."

"Fine, and one more thing. I think one of those cowboys is fooling around with my niece. See what you can do about that, will you?"

"Sure thing," Slocum replied. "As soon as I finish my dessert."

3

As always, dinner for the ranch hands was served in the bunkhouse. The front section of the long, flat building was occupied by a large table and several chairs where the hired help could eat without disturbing the Singers themselves. Seeing as how Hal Singer blustered even more over his meals, the hands knew they were getting the better end of this bargain. Even though Slocum's meal was cold, it still beat the hell out of sharing it with Hal.

"I can put some of this under a fire if you like," Kelly Singer offered.

Slocum shook his head while gnawing on some lukewarm steak. "This is just fine," he said through a mouthful of food. "I'll take some more coffee, though."

Kelly smiled and got up to walk to the smaller table beside the bunkhouse's front door. A pot of coffee stood there, so she refilled Slocum's cup and brought it back to him. "Whatever you said to my uncle got him riled up," she told him with a crooked grin.

"I just told him what happened when I went after those rustlers," he replied. Then, with a smirk, he added, "And I may have put him in his place a little. Couldn't help myself."

"We all try to put him in his place now and then. It never seems to stick, though."

"Did Robbie get settled in?"

"I think so. I didn't go over to check on him, but I didn't hear any shooting or yelling, so things must be in order."

Slocum thought about that for a few seconds. "Maybe. Maybe not. I'll go have a look for myself."

Kelly placed her hand on Slocum's arm and rubbed it gently. "Don't take too long. I've got plans for you, mister."

Reflexively, Slocum glanced about. The back section of the bunkhouse was divided into several small rooms by partitions that didn't reach all the way to the ceiling. Therefore, sound tended to travel throughout the whole building. Even though Slocum wasn't concerned about the consequences if his nights with Kelly were discovered, he didn't exactly want them to become common knowledge either. Since every hired hand on the ranch seemed to have their eye on the tall redhead, being known as the luckiest one of the bunch could make working with them needlessly difficult. More than that, however, Slocum didn't want to jeopardize any future paydays if Hal got wind of it. At the moment, Slocum and Kelly seemed to be the only ones moving about inside the entire building, but he kept his voice down all the same.

"I'm riding out again soon," he told her.

Kelly's sly grin flipped over into a perfectly curved frown. "How soon?"

"Early tomorrow morning. Probably before dawn, since I want to get out to the Landry spread close to first light."

"Can't you get there a little later? You know I like waking up with you, and nobody even notices my own bed is empty until breakfast is served."

Slocum tapped his finger against Kelly's mouth and said, "I bet that face just melts the old man's heart."

Slowly, the well-practiced frown gave way to a more natural grin. "More or less."

"Well, this is a business matter and the only reason I'm dealing with it at all is because you kept me so preoccupied when I should have been riding along the fence line."

"You didn't seem to mind when I was riding you."

"No, I didn't," Slocum replied. "That's my fault and I don't intend on letting that happen again."

"What do you care? They're not your cows."

"Maybe not, but I was hired to do a job and I'll see it through. Once I fix my mistake, I'll be putting this ranch behind me for good."

"You're going to leave me?" Kelly asked as her perfect frown returned.

Slocum got up, brushed some hair away from Kelly's face, and told her, "I sure am, but I don't intend on leaving without one more taste of dessert. If you've got a sweet tooth, you know where to find me." With that, Slocum walked out of the bunkhouse and headed for the stables.

It was a short walk, but it allowed him to enjoy some crisp night air. The cool beef and cooler potatoes were settling like rocks in his stomach. By the time he got to the stables, however, Slocum was feeling better. It helped to see a few men who were doing a whole lot worse.

The kid and Brady were still wrapped up with the same ropes Slocum had used to tie them up in the first place. The pair sat with their backs to each other and a post in between them. After a moment, Slocum realized there was another layer of ropes going around the men and the post to form one neat package.

"Not taking any chances, huh, Robbie?" Slocum asked as he approached the ranch hand.

Robbie was only one of four hired hands inside the stables. Those men, along with the outlaws and the horses, made the stables feel especially crowded. To add to the tension in there, each of the ranch hands was armed. Robbie held a shotgun cradled in his arms, and nearly jumped out of his skin when Slocum approached.

"Don't sneak up on me like that, Slocum!" Robbie snapped.

"I wasn't sneaking. Have these two been giving you any trouble?"

"No."

Looking over at the man-sized bundle in the corner that was covered by a tarp, Slocum asked, "What about that one?"

Robbie glanced over at the bundle and quickly looked away. "No."

"Then why are you all so jumpy?"

"Because we ain't used to guarding prisoners, that's why."

All Slocum needed to do was look around at the other hired hands to see the same anxiety reflected on all those faces. "Maybe you should start by feeding the prisoners. They're looking a little pale."

"A trip to the goddamn outhouse would be in order," Brady snarled.

Slocum nodded. "He's right. Although they couldn't make this place smell any worse."

"Go to hell!" the kid growled.

Fixing a mean stare on both outlaws, Slocum asked, "Who took the bandannas from their mouths?"

"We thought it'd make it easier for them to breathe," Robbie said.

"They won't need to breathe at all if we put them under a tarp like their friend in the corner over there."

After both outlaws looked toward the body of their partner, they shut their mouths and lowered their eyes.

Slocum pulled Robbie aside and spoke in a whisper that wouldn't make it back to the prisoners. "See to it that these men are fed and watered. And unless you want them to get a whole lot messier, I'd show them to an outhouse as well."

"But," Robbie asked nervously, "won't that mean untying them?"

"Yeah, but I'll lend a hand with that and then make certain they get tied up again."

Since that seemed to be exactly what the ranch hand had been after, Robbie nodded enthusiastically. "That'd be good. But why go through so much trouble? I mean, why didn't you just ride them into Westlake and drop them off at the sheriff's?"

"How long of a ride is it from here to Westlake?" Slocum asked.

"Doesn't take more than a few hours."

"And from where I caught them, it would have been another couple hours on top of that. I was tired and hungry and knew you boys would be more than happy to lend me a hand in seeing these men safely to the law. In fact, I thought you might volunteer to take them in yourselves since I have to pay Landry a visit in the morning."

Robbie let out a groan. "I ain't never done anything like this. Ain't it dangerous?"

"No more dangerous than hauling any other load. The only difference is that if this load gives you any trouble, you shoot it." Seeing the wary grin on Robbie's face, Slocum slapped him on the back and added, "You'll be fine. There may be a reward coming for those thieves and if there is, you can take a share for yourself. I'll take another share and save some of it for Hal. Just be sure to tell him it's half. Now let's get this messy business over with."

The messy business turned out to be quick and painless. With Slocum overseeing the process, the two outlaws were given some food that was even colder than Slocum's steak, followed by a few ladles of water and a trip to the outhouse. Brady and the kid muttered a few threats, but weren't quite up to the task of backing them up.

After retying the ropes and cinching the knots, Slocum double-checked to make certain the outlaws wouldn't be going anywhere. The task of watching the outlaws was divided among the men, and Slocum volunteered for the last shift. Robbie took first watch, so Slocum had no problem

leaving the outlaws in his hands. From there, Slocum mean-
dered toward the bunkhouse, circled around to the back of
the Singer home, and wound up in a shed that was set apart
from the others.

The carriage house was big enough to hold three wagons
as well as a few carts. At the moment, it only held one carriage with a broken wheel and a smaller cart that was in
good repair, but dusty enough to have spent at least three
winters without seeing the outdoors. There was one large
door that was kept locked, and a smaller door on the side,
which was usually locked as well. Slocum tested the handle
of the smaller door and found he could pull it open easily
enough.

Inside, Kelly Singer waited for him on her knees behind
the wagon with the broken wheel. Her pale skin was illu-
minated by the dull flicker of a single lantern. She wore a
black corset that was cinched tightly around her body to
keep her plump breasts held up so the tops of her large
pink nipples spilled over the top. Her red hair was tied into
a single tail that flowed down her back and exposed the
supple lines of her neck and ears.

"I was hoping you didn't forget about me," she whispered. "You took a long time to get here."

Slocum shut the door and walked to her. The floor of the
carriage house was littered with everything from bolts and
nails to rusted pieces of seat springs and brackets. After a
few steps, however, he reached the spot that he and Kelly
had claimed for their own. It was cleared off and covered
by a thick blanket.

"There was work that needed to be done," he said as he
unbuckled his gun belt.

Kelly stood up to show Slocum the boots she wore, which
were laced all the way up to her knees. "There's still work to
be done," she said. "Now come over here and do it."

Dropping his gun belt to the edge of the blanket where
he could still get to it if the need arose, Slocum placed his

hands on Kelly's hips and kissed her deeply. She melted in his arms and moaned softly as he pressed his lips against hers. In moments, she responded by slipping her tongue into his mouth and rubbing her leg along his thigh.

Having spent plenty of nights with her, Slocum knew what Kelly wanted. In fact, every time they got together, she seemed to want more. Perhaps it was because Hal Singer and every other man on that ranch treated her like a princess. Kelly spent most of her days lapping up that treatment the way a cat lapped up warm milk, but she trembled at the first hint that Slocum's touch might get a little rough.

After the kiss had gone on long enough for Slocum to feel a response of his own, he pulled her even closer. His arms locked around her waist, making it impossible for her to get free. She writhed against him and wrapped her arms around him while her breathing grew heavier and heavier. When she finally leaned her head back, she pulled in a labored breath and growled, "You kept me waiting on purpose, didn't you?"

"I thought about not coming here at all," Slocum replied, figuring that would get to her even more.

Judging by the way Kelly's breaths deepened, he was right.

"You'd never leave without saying a proper good-bye," she sighed.

"Maybe I'm saying good-bye now. I do have to get my sleep."

Kelly's eyes widened with the challenge she'd been given. "You're not going anywhere," she told him. "Not until I'm through with you." Kelly pushed away from Slocum and pulled his jeans open. She dropped to her knees, taking his jeans down as well. Grabbing his rigid penis with one hand, she wrapped her lips around it as if she was devouring her last meal. When Slocum placed his hands on the back of her head, she sucked him even harder.

As Kelly's full, soft lips slid up and down along his

length, Slocum smiled and leaned back to enjoy it. He used his hand to guide her, but she didn't need much instruction. Ever since he'd figured out how the redhead was strung, he'd played her like a fiddle. Of course, it was just as possible that she was plucking *his* strings. Considering how well the arrangement had worked out for both of them, neither was about to complain.

Kelly's lips and tongue worked in perfect harmony as they slid up and down his cock. No matter how many times she sucked on him, Slocum never got used to just how good she was at the job. She knew just when to slow down or speed up. She knew when to suck harder and when to just let her tongue slide against the bottom of his shaft. When she took him completely in her mouth, she moaned just enough to get him even harder.

Before he was pushed too far, Slocum eased her back and helped her to her feet. "Get up against that wall," he said.

Eyes flashing at the brusque demand, Kelly backed up until her shoulders bumped against the side of the shed. She kept her wide eyes on him and gasped expectantly when Slocum reached out to pull one of her legs up to his waist level. She shifted her weight and balanced on her other leg as she reached out to stroke his rigid pole.

"I want you to fuck me from behind," she whispered. "If this is the last night you're here, I want that one more time."

"You'll get what I give you," Slocum said.

And just as he'd thought she would, Kelly let out an excited moan. "Yes, John. Just don't make me wait."

Holding her leg up, Slocum pushed his hips forward until his cock brushed against the warm spot between her thighs. Kelly was already wet and the more he teased her, the wetter she got. By the time he allowed the tip of his cock to part the soft lips of her pussy, they were both ready to burst. Slocum entered her less than halfway, but that was still enough to make Kelly's next breath catch in her throat. He thrust a bit farther into her and immediately felt her start to shake.

Slocum grinned and watched the changes move over Kelly's face. First, she was anxious. Then, she grew impatient. Before long, she simply reveled in the feeling of his hardness inside her and waited for Slocum to finally bury his cock all the way into her. When that moment came, her smile returned as well.

With both of them standing up, he entered her from an angle that sent shivers throughout Kelly's entire body. Slocum pumped in and out a few times before grinding his hips in a slow circle. Just when Kelly seemed to have trouble drawing another breath, he raised her leg a little higher. Kelly's eyes snapped open wide and her mouth hung open as Slocum reached yet another spot inside her. For a few moments, she couldn't move. Then, as she became accustomed to the new position, she slipped one hand behind his neck and used the other to brace herself against the wall.

As soon as Slocum felt her wiggle her hips, he knew she was ready. He cupped her rounded backside in both hands and thrust his hips back and forth. Before long, he could feel her supporting her own weight on one leg while hooking her other around his waist. As Slocum gained momentum, he ran a hand along her calf, easing it along her thigh while pumping into her harder and faster.

"Oh, Jesus," Kelly groaned as she clawed at him as well as the wall behind her. "Just like that, John. Just like that."

Slocum thrust into her again and again. He could feel her pussy tightening around him as she clenched her eyes shut and let a powerful orgasm sweep through her. He slowed down for a few seconds, but moved even faster when she finally started to relax. As soon as he felt her body start to slump, he lowered her leg and allowed her to stand on her own.

Pulling back just enough to slip out of her, Slocum said, "Now turn around."

"I don't . . . I don't think I can take any more," Kelly sighed.

"You sure about that?"

Slowly, she opened her eyes. After catching her breath, Kelly turned around and placed both hands flat against the wall. When she arched her back, her plump buttocks stood up proudly.

Slocum let his eyes wander up from there until he could see the thick red ponytail dangling from the back of her head to tease the bare skin between her shoulders. Although he reached around to cup her breasts, Slocum didn't bother to remove her corset. In fact, the single piece of clothing she wore did wonders to make the rest of her body look even better. That section of constricting material made her waist the perfect shape for his hands, and her bare bottom seemed rounder and more inviting. By the time Slocum stepped close enough to run his cock between her legs, he was harder than he'd ever been.

Kelly spread her legs apart a little more and looked back at him. She didn't say a word as he guided his rigid penis into her as far as he could. She let out a slow breath, closed her eyes, and shifted her hips slowly back and forth.

Thanks to the heels of Kelly's boots, Slocum was able to enter her perfectly from behind. He maintained his grip on her hips and pumped into her a few times. With every stroke, her pussy got wetter and gripped him until she climaxed again.

Slocum didn't want to prolong it any further. He probably couldn't have even if he tried. Rather than fight what was coming, he extended his arms to cup her breasts while thrusting in and out of her with building fury.

Kelly leaned against the wall until she was practically clawing at the wood.

Slocum grabbed her and buried his cock in her one more time before he finally exploded.

When he started pulling his clothes on, Slocum couldn't help but notice the frown had returned to Kelly's face.

"You're really leaving?" she asked.

"Yep."

"Then," Kelly whispered as she let her hands wander down to the glistening patch of hair between her legs, "I'll have to take care of myself."

Slocum needed his sleep, but he stayed up with Kelly in that carriage house. There would be plenty of time to sleep when he was dead.

4

The first light of dawn was barely showing in the sky as Slocum rode away from the Singer Moon Ranch. Despite a very active night, he had managed to get a few winks of sleep before Kelly had to sneak back to her own room in the family house. That left him with enough time to check on the prisoners while collecting his horse.

Brady and the kid were slumped forward, dead asleep, when Slocum found them. The ranch hand guarding them sat perched on the edge of a chair with a shotgun in his lap as if he was keeping an eye on the devil himself.

"You comin' back, Mr. Slocum?" the ranch hand asked.

"I suppose I am," Slocum had replied. "Hal's gonna want to know how my talk with Landry went, but I'm sure you and the rest of the boys can see these men safely to Westlake."

The ranch hand did nothing to hide the nervousness on his face. He tightened his grip on his shotgun and then turned back around to guard the sleeping men.

As Slocum rode, he shook his head. Somehow, he'd tricked himself into thinking he'd be putting the ranch behind him for good. Having reminded himself that he needed to come back at least once made him feel anxious all over again. It wasn't that the Singer Moon was a bad place. It wasn't even that Hal didn't pay well. It was just that the ranch was a single place in a larger world that was tugging awfully hard on Slocum's reins.

There was plenty of money to be made at that ranch, and a man like Hal Singer could come up with plenty of jobs for him to do. In the end, it all boiled down to the fact that Slocum hadn't intended on staying put for half as long as he already had. Now, every day he spent in the same place felt like he was digging himself into a deeper trench.

The ride to the Landry spread wasn't too long, but it covered a lot of open ground and plenty of beautiful terrain. The Arizona Territory was always a sight to behold, but that sight was even better in the earliest hours of the day. As the sun inched its way up into the sky, the colors that washed down onto the ground varied from deep purples to dark reds. The clouds were just taking on an orange hue as Slocum caught his first glimpse of the fence sectioning off Landry's property. He could have jumped a low spot in that fence to catch some attention real quick, but Slocum opted to follow it to the main gate. Even though he'd opted for the more polite route, Slocum still attracted some attention from Landry's hired hands. By the time he reached the ranch's main gate, there was a group of three armed men waiting there for him.

"I'm here to see Mr. Landry," Slocum announced.

The men at the gate looked at him as if they were trying to guess the weight of a dung pile. Finally, one of them asked, "Who are you?"

"My name's John Slocum."

"And what's this about?"

"Are you Mr. Landry?"

The spokesman of the group blinked and replied, "No."

"Then my business isn't with you."

The scowl on the spokesman's face grew darker as he turned his horse to make certain Slocum could see the gun hanging from his waist. "If you want to set foot on this property, your business is with me. If you don't want to state it, then you can go piss up a rope."

"All right. It's about the cattle Mr. Landry stole."

All three of Landry's men bristled when they heard that. They also shifted their hands a bit closer to the weapons they were carrying. No guns were aimed at Slocum just yet, but it was only a matter of time before that would change.

"I suppose you got proof to back up that claim?" the spokesman asked.

Slocum nodded. "I sure do, and something tells me Mr. Landry will want to keep it between me and him. Now, if you'd like to answer to your boss as to why you were in on that conversation, you go right ahead. Or, if you're already involved in it, you know exactly what I'm talking about. Either way, I don't have to tell you another goddamn thing."

Like most tough talkers, the other men backed down once their bluff had been called. Slocum had no way of knowing if those men were directly involved with Hal's missing cattle, but the shiftiness of their eyes betrayed more than a hint of a guilty conscience.

"Come along with us then," the spokesman replied. "But you'll hand over that pistol."

"If you want it, you can come and take it," Slocum growled.

None of the men were eager to take him up on that offer. Since the spokesman fell into that group, he grudgingly waved Slocum through the gate.

Slocum rode alongside the spokesman, with the other two men taking positions either beside him or behind him. It wasn't the most ideal arrangement for Slocum, but he knew he wasn't bound to get a better one anytime soon. The fact that he was on Landry's property meant there could be men anywhere at all lining up a rifle shot or getting to a spot where they could attack him. If Landry wanted Slocum dead, he would have his chance to take his crack at him. All

Slocum could do was keep his eyes and ears open and his hand within easy reach of his cross-draw holster.

The ride across the Landry spread was fairly quick and very quiet. None of the men spoke to Slocum, and he wasn't interested in striking up a conversation with any of them. Along the way, Slocum got a look at plenty of open ground, some fences, and a few sheds scattered here and there. As far as ranches went, it was nothing out of the ordinary. One thing that did strike him, however, was the lack of cattle.

There were a few head grazing on some grass here and there, but not nearly the numbers he would expect on a spread working to its capacity. Slocum didn't know if Landry was between drives, but the fact that there were some animals to be seen made him certain the rustlers' information had been correct. Landry had acquired a few cattle recently, and the rest of his herd was either sold or kept separated from the ones Slocum had already seen. Since Slocum doubted he'd be allowed to get a look at the brands on those cattle, he guessed Landry would fill in the gaps when he spoke to him face-to-face.

The buildings situated toward the middle of the property looked similar to Singer's. There was a barn, a stable, a bunkhouse, and a smaller family home. The sizes may have varied a bit, but not by much. As far as Slocum was concerned, if you'd seen one ranch, you'd pretty much seen them all. Not every ranch, however, came equipped with so many armed men posted on the house's front porch.

As Slocum was led to what looked to be the family home, he counted half a dozen men brandishing rifles or shotguns. They flanked a taller fellow wearing a gray waistcoat, who stood on the porch with his hands clasped behind his back. By the time Slocum pulled back on his reins, the tall man in the waistcoat had already stepped down from the porch to approach the new arrivals.

"Good morning," the tall man said. "I wasn't expecting a visitor today."

"Well, you got one. My name's John Slocum. I've been working at the Singer Moon Ranch."

"Yeah?"

"Yeah," Slocum continued in the same cordial tone he'd used to introduce himself. "Are you Mr. Landry?"

"Sure enough."

"Then I'd like a moment of your time to discuss a thing or two."

"I don't have a lot of moments to spare nowadays. Things haven't exactly been quiet around here."

"I think Hal Singer is of that very same opinion."

"Hal ain't the one under a curse!" Landry spat as he swung an arm toward his barn.

Slocum looked in the direction that Landry had waved to, and found the same barn he'd spotted on his way to the house. Now that he was a little closer, however, Slocum could also see the peculiar symbols painted across the barn doors. The doors were open a ways, but the design was fairly easy to put together. The writing across the top of the barn just below the roof wasn't quite so clear.

"Is that a star?" Slocum asked.

"It's supposed to ward off . . ." Landry cut himself short and winced as if he'd literally bitten his tongue. "Yeah."

"What's the rest of it?"

"Why don't you ask Singer? Since he's the one who paid for this damned curse, he should be able to tell you all about it."

Slocum squinted at the barn, but couldn't make any more sense out of what he saw. Shaking his head, he looked back at the man in the waistcoat. "I don't know about any curses, but I do know about missing cattle."

"What's that to me?"

"I have reliable sources that tell me you're the one who had Hal's cows stolen."

"And what sources might those be?" Landry asked defiantly.

Looking around at the armed men that were closing in around him, Slocum replied, "For starters, I've got the rustlers themselves. They put up a fight, but started talking once they found themselves on the losing end. From then on, they've had plenty to say. You want me to air it all out here or should we talk man-to-man?"

"I should air your guts out just for you comin' onto my land and calling me a goddamn thief!"

"You could," Slocum replied, "but that wouldn't keep those rustlers from talking. They're tucked away nice and safe for the moment. If I don't come back, those men might be ridden over to tell their tales to whatever passes for law around here."

Landry pulled in a breath and chewed on it for a few seconds. His teeth ground together and the muscles in his face twitched beneath his skin. When he let out his breath, he sounded like he was pushing steam through a piston. "Fine. We'll talk out back. You ain't settin' foot in my home and you ain't stayin' for any longer than need be."

"Fine with me."

Slocum swung down from his saddle and looped his reins around the post that bordered the porch. He kept his steps slow and easy, despite all the guns that were on display for his benefit. When he met the glance of a fellow wielding a double-barreled shotgun, Slocum tipped his hat and kept on walking.

Landry walked around the side of the house, which looked like it would have belonged on any homestead that was built for any family in nearly any place where there was land to be farmed. Once Slocum checked to make sure there were no guns being aimed at him from any of the windows, he shifted his eyes elsewhere. What caught his attention first was the barn and stables that were built fairly close together.

Other than the symbols he'd already seen, Slocum spotted a few other oddities about the barn. There were strings dangling from the door and loft window with things tied to them that rattled in the breeze. The stables also had crude stars painted on the doors, but had even more symbols painted around the door's frame. When the wind blew, those strings rattled, but no other sounds came from that direction.

"So Hal's missing a few cows, huh?" Landry asked as he planted his feet and crossed his arms over his chest.

"Not missing," Slocum pointed out. "Stolen."

"Well, it serves him right for what he did to me."

"And what was that?"

Nodding toward the barn and stable, Landry asked, "See that?"

"I don't know exactly what I'm looking at, but yeah, I see it."

"I'll tell you what it is. All that shit is to ward off the hex that was put on this place. The woman who keeps my house clean is superstitious enough to know what to paint to keep a curse from spreading any further and maybe killing off my family."

Slocum tried to keep from laughing, but couldn't prevent a bit of a chuckle from coming out.

"Real goddamn funny, huh?" Landry growled. "That's what I thought, too. Then my pigs got sick. Not just a few of them, mind you. All of 'em."

"Pigs get sick sometimes."

"That's what I thought, too. Then the cows started falling ill."

"So, you've never lost any livestock to sickness?" Slocum asked.

"Of course I have. Every farmer has. Every rancher loses a certain percentage to bad health or bad weather. Once that percentage gets too high, it's got to be somethin' more than that."

"Or it could just be a bad season. That's been known to happen, too. No amount of painting on your walls can help with that."

Landry looked over at Slocum and then fixed his eyes back on his barn. "You think I'm crazy?"

"No. I think you arranged to trim some of Hal Singer's herd. That's the only reason I'm here."

"I only took what that bastard owes me," Landry stated. "Considering how much that witch of his cost me, I'd say he got off light."

"Now there's a witch?"

"Come along with me if you think I'm so goddamn crazy," Landry said as he stormed toward the barn.

Slocum thought of a few things to say just to steer the talk back in the proper direction, but went along with Landry instead. He couldn't recall ever hearing so much talk about witches and curses unless it was part of some campfire story. As he trailed along behind Landry, Slocum found himself getting curious as to just what the hell the man would say next. He certainly wasn't expecting to see what Landry showed him.

The pile of dead meat and splintered bones might have formerly been a cow or a bull or even a small horse. There was also the possibility that it was several smaller carcasses piled together and left in the sun. All Slocum knew for certain was that the carnage behind the barn was swarming with flies and stank like hell.

"Jesus," Slocum grunted as he slapped a hand over his mouth and nose. "What the hell is that?"

"That's some of my livestock!" Landry exclaimed.

"Then bury it, for Christ's sake!"

"I did, but it winds up aboveground the next morning."

"Then you've got coyotes," Slocum said. "Or cats or . . . God knows however many other animals that would be attracted to a kill that's fresh or otherwise. How does this lead to you stealing from Hal Singer and calling it even?"

Even though the air was thick with the smell of rotten meat and alive with hundreds of flying insects, Landry stood in the middle of it as if he'd been raised there. He barely even swatted the flies away from his mouth as he shouted, "That son of a bitch hired a witch to curse my ranch! He told me he was gonna do it! I laughed in his face, but look and see what happened! Just look at it!"

"All I see is some dead animals that need to go into a hole deep enough to keep away scavengers."

"All right then. Come take a look at this." Landry stormed away from the carcasses, and Slocum was all too happy to follow. He walked straight across to the stables and pointed toward the open rear doors. "Take a look at that."

Even before they'd gotten to the stable, Slocum could see a few horses milling about outside the building. When he looked inside through the doors, he saw nothing out of the ordinary. In fact, the stalls looked clean and in good repair. A few tools hung from the walls and some hay was stacked neatly along one wall. Shifting his eyes back to Landry, he said, "Looks in proper order to me."

"Right," Landry snapped with a nod. "Then why the hell won't my horses go anywhere near it?"

"They're right there."

"Yes. *Outside* the stable. You so much as move a muscle to lead them in there and they'll bolt all the way to the Pacific Ocean. I nearly lost every horse I own, which would'a cost me more than you're paid in a decade! If my boys hadn't rounded 'em up and got them situated outside, I still wouldn't have anything to pull my wagon into town."

"So that's why those horses were stolen along with the cattle?" Slocum asked.

Without batting an eye, Landry replied, "You're goddamn right. And if Hal Singer wants his property back, he can call off that goddamn witch."

Slocum stood and examined the stables before casting his eyes toward the horses milling around outside. He didn't see anything particularly odd until he looked back at Landry's wide eyes and flushed face. The rancher was nearly foaming at the mouth.

Before Slocum said anything that would make things worse, he filled his lungs and emptied them in a calm sigh. "I've been working with Hal Singer for a while now, and I've never heard a thing about any witch."

"You think he's gonna make it common knowledge?"

"I suppose not, but—"

"You ride back and ask him about her. He'll tell you!"

"All right. Now I see what this is," Slocum said. "I ride back to Hal with this bullshit and then he sends me back here. Meanwhile, you've got plenty of time to cover your tracks regarding those rustlers and the stolen cattle. What's the matter, Landry? You just need another day or so to change the brands on those cows you bought?"

"I ain't covering any tracks," Landry said. "I took them cows and I took them horses. They're repayment for what was taken from me."

"Taken by disease or . . ." Once again, Slocum stopped short of making the situation worse. He knew he wouldn't have the patience to pull back the reins for much longer, though. "I came here to give you a chance to put this straight before things got messy."

"You wanna bring the law up here? The sheriff knows about that witch just like most anyone else in Westlake knows about her."

"Then why haven't I heard about her?" Slocum asked.

"Because," Landry replied in a harsh whisper, "it ain't the sort of thing that good, God-fearing folks talk about."

"It's not the sort of thing anyone talks about unless they've been kicked in the head by a mule or are running one hell of a fever."

"I don't give a dog's ass what you think of me. I got animals that drop over for no good reason, horses that can smell that witch's curse where they sleep, and fertile ground that sprouts nothin' but weeds. Why don't you go take a look at what used to be my pastures to see some more of that witch's handiwork?"

Slocum nodded. "All right. I'll go have a look. I'll take a nice tour of your property while I round up Hal Singer's cattle. If those are more of his horses, I'll be taking them, too."

Landry's face was a blank slate. All the anger that had been there before was washed away and his eyes took on a cold sheen. "You won't take a damn thing from me. I lost enough already."

"That doesn't give you the right to steal from anyone else."

"Then go on and fetch the sheriff. Fetch the goddamn federal army and whoever else you want."

Slocum could see the armed men closing in on him, but that didn't stop him from stepping right up to Landry and looking him in the eye. Even though he could now see that Landry himself was armed, Slocum stared him down and said, "I have an easier time believing in witches than I do an honest lawman. When I rode out here, it was to put this matter to rest. I was hired to do a job and I'd prefer to do it properly. I didn't intend on spilling blood for Hal Singer, but I also won't be chased off anyone's land by some fucking ghost story. On top of that, you just plain irritate me, Mr. Landry."

"I won't have anyone speak to me like that on my property."

"Trust me, I can think of plenty worse things to say. Point me toward those stolen cows and I'll thank you kindly. If you've got more witch talk to air out, then keep it to yourself."

Landry's eyes narrowed and his hand twitched toward the gun that was kept in a shoulder holster under his waistcoat. Rather than draw his own shooting iron, he snapped, "Someone get this son of a bitch out of my sight."

Slocum took a step back, which allowed him to get a better look at the men that were closest to him. In the space of a second, he could pick out a few who looked too nervous to speak, and a couple that were shocked to see things get pushed so far. That left two men that could be a problem. One of them was a big fellow with a pistol, who looked more than ready to use it. The other was the stout man with dark hair and a shotgun who'd been eyeballing Slocum ever since the front gate. That one brought his weapon to his shoulder and prepared to fire.

Slocum's response to that was to draw his Colt Navy and aim from the hip. Fortunately, the man with the shotgun was stout enough and close enough to be an easy target. The gun in Slocum's hand barked once and sent a chunk of hot lead through the man's chest.

"That's another one for the pile," Slocum announced. "Anyone else want to join him?"

Slocum didn't have to look at the men for long before he figured out one thing for certain: They might have all been armed, but they were ranchers and not killers. Already, those men carried their weapons as if they were sorry they'd ever picked them up in the first place.

Keeping his gun in hand, Slocum moved toward his horse. "I can see myself out."

5

When Slocum arrived back at the Singer Moon Ranch, he wasn't alone.

As with all the other times he approached the ranch, he was spotted before too long and escorts came along to meet him. Unlike his approach to the Landry ranch, however, the few escorts that got to Slocum's side weren't hostile.

"I was about to ride out to meet up with you, Slocum," Robbie said. "I didn't like the notion of you heading out there on yer own."

"Why not? You didn't seem to have a problem with it before."

Slocum's words stung just as much as he'd meant them to. However, as soon as Robbie turned his head away, Slocum felt like an ass for saying them. Dulling the edge in his voice, Slocum added, "But someone had to stay behind and watch those rustlers. Did someone already take them to town?"

"Uhh . . . not exactly."

Slocum rode through the ranch's gate, and finally let out the breath he'd been holding. During the entire ride back, he'd figured some of Landry's men would be following him. So far, he'd been lucky. Now that he was back on

46

Singer's property, he guessed anyone trying to sneak up on him would be spotted.

Although Robbie hadn't spotted any bushwhackers, he had spotted something else. "What are those?" he asked as he stared at the trail behind Slocum.

Turning in his saddle, Slocum looked back and replied, "Looks an awful lot like cows to me."

"Are those our cows?"

"Some of them. I was in a hurry when I left the Landry spread, but I rounded up as many as I could. It wasn't easy on my own. Looks like I might have lost a few along the way. It's all right, though," Slocum added as he turned back around to face Robbie. "I just took what I could find, so most of them are probably Landry's."

Robbie looked around at the other hired hands that had accompanied him to the fence line, and all of them started to laugh. "You're a crazy son of a bitch, Slocum. You know that?"

"I've been called worse. You think you boys can round up those cattle without my help?"

"I suppose we can manage." With that, Robbie snapped his reins and rode out to circle the group of cattle that had been following Slocum like a gaggle of geese. There weren't many of them and after a bit of riding, the hands picked up a few stragglers who'd wandered away from Slocum before reaching the Singer Moon. After collecting what they could, the cowboys raced back to the ranch so they could hear what other trouble Slocum had stirred up while he was away.

"So," Hal said as he opened a box on his desk and selected a cheroot as if it was somehow the best of the bunch, "let's hear what Landry had to say."

Slocum shrugged and replied, "He's the one that hired those rustlers."

"You're sure of it?"

"As sure as I can be."

Hal grinned from ear to ear and turned the box on his desk around so it faced Slocum. "Have a smoke, my good man. You've earned it."

Although Slocum wasn't as honored as Hal seemed to think he should be, he reached into the box and took one of the cheroots from the top of the stack. The moment he struck a match and lit it, Slocum realized why the rancher was rarely seen without one. The tobacco was expensive and had a smooth, rich flavor. The longer the smoke rolled around in his mouth, the better it got. When Slocum blew the smoke out, he was sad to see it go.

"That's not bad," Slocum said as he held the cheroot out in front of him.

"Only the best. Now tell me how you got that smug bastard to confess."

"I asked him if he hired those men."

After waiting for a few seconds with his eyebrows raised, Hal asked, "That's it?"

"That's it."

"And he just confessed to being a cattle rustler?"

"Well, he confessed to hiring cattle rustlers," Slocum explained. "I suppose there's not too much of a difference."

Shaking his head, Hal said, "No, there sure isn't. I'm sure Sheriff Bilson will love to hear about this. I don't suppose you got anything that might hold up in a court of law?"

"There was one other thing that Landry talked about. Although I don't think it's exactly the sort of thing I'd take in front of a judge."

"What's that?"

Slocum took another puff from the cheroot and sent a smoky breath into the air as he fixed his eyes on Hal and said, "Landry says he took those animals to repay the damage done to him by you."

"Damage, huh?"

Nodding, Slocum continued to watch the man. He especially wanted to see Hal's reaction when he told him, "Landry says you hired a witch to curse his place."

What bothered Slocum the most was the fact that Hal wasn't rattled by the accusation. In fact, if Slocum was a betting man, he might have put money on the notion that Hal was somewhat expecting to hear those very words.

"That's plum ridiculous," Hal muttered without very much conviction.

As much as Slocum agreed with the sentiment, he kept his voice steady and said, "His barn was marked up with some peculiar symbols."

"Superstitious farmers have been buying into that nonsense for centuries," Hal was quick to point out.

"There was also a pile of dead animals that he says were stricken by the curse. His horses bolt from their own stables and he's having a hell of a time getting them to stay put."

If Hal tried to cover his interest, he did a bad job of it. "Is that so?" he asked with the slightest hint of a grin at one corner of his mouth.

Slocum nodded. "He even says his grazing land is drying up so much that it's damn near unusable."

Hal's eyes flicked to Slocum as he asked, "Did you see that for yourself?"

"I saw something like it," Slocum replied, "but the property could just be poorly looked after. So you think he's full of smoke?"

"Don't you?"

Slocum took the cheroot from his mouth and used it to point squarely at the rancher. "You're the one that matters here. Did you do something to poison Landry's animals or ruin his land?"

"Me? No."

"That's funny, because you've got the same stupid smirk on your face that Landry had when I asked if he stole your animals. It turned out he hired someone for the job so he could step back and pretend to be innocent. Is that what's going on here?"

Hal chomped on the end of his cheroot as if he was trying to eat it. Turning around to look at his property through the window behind his desk, he said, "I already told you the bullshit Landry's been trying to pull. That's not even the half of it. There's been—"

"I don't give a damn about your neighborly disputes," Slocum cut in. "What I can't believe is that a couple of grown men are seriously discussing witches. The fact that I'm one of those men is even worse!"

"I don't know what you'd call her, but that woman is a witch in my book," Hal said.

"Why? Does she mix up concoctions and sell them with all sorts of promises attached? I know plenty of salesmen who do the same thing without being called witches."

"She does more than that." As Hal spoke, his eyes started to wander as though he was afraid of fixing them in one particular spot. He shifted from one foot to the other and then moved away from the window. "I'm not the only one who believes it. Hell, go see her for yourself if you think I'm so crazy."

Slocum waved that away with the same hand he used to hold his cheroot. "I don't need to see any old woman to tell you she's no witch. If you and this whole damn county want to believe that nonsense, you all go right ahead. At least a spectacle like that will make what I did seem like nothing at all."

"What did you do?" Hal asked. "More than what you already told me?"

"I took some of Landry's cows."

"Were they mine?"

"I didn't stop to check every brand," Slocum said. "When I left there, I was riled up and just took whatever I could get."

"Landry does tend to have that effect on folks."

"Yeah. Especially when he threatens to kill me."

Hal twitched when he heard that, but part of that seemed like the prelude to a grin. "Set his hired guns on you, did he?"

"He tried. He's short one gunhand, though."

"How bad did you hurt the man?" Hal asked.

"Bad enough to put him in the ground. I figured you might want to know in case the subject arose. Anyway, I intend on moving along, so you won't have to worry about looking after me. If anyone asks, just tell them I was gone before you knew what happened."

"No need to run, Slocum. If you were defending yourself, you don't have to worry about anything. Landry ain't exactly known for being levelheaded. Anyone who knows that prick already knows he's got plenty of killers on his payroll."

"First of all," Slocum replied, "those men were as close to killers as the men you got working for you. They're armed, for sure, but I'd wager the last thing any of them killed was a horse with a broken leg. And second, I'm not running. I'm just putting some distance between myself and a big load of crazy men."

Rather than be offended by that, Hal simply smiled a bit wider. He even walked around his desk to rest a hand on Slocum's shoulder. "Don't get all upset. This mess turned a little worse than I thought it would, but you've done a hell of a job for me. I intend on sticking by a man who does that kind of good work."

Slocum looked down at the hand on his shoulder with enough intensity to burn through it. Once Hal got the message and pulled his arm back, Slocum told him, "Thanks, but no, thanks. I've been meaning to move along for a while."

"Where are you headed?"

"Away from here. That's all you need to know."

"Fine," Hal said as he raised both hands as though he

was being robbed at gunpoint. "I'm not about to hold you prisoner."

"That's right. And you're not about to get out of paying me the last of the money you owe me."

"Hal Singer may be a lot of things, but he ain't no liar. I said I'd pay you and I will."

"All right then. Give me my money and I'll be on my way."

Hal winced, placed the cheroot back in his mouth, and gnawed on it.

"What is it?" Slocum growled.

"I promised you a good amount of money. The only problem is that I just paid the rest of my hands and I don't have the cash here. That is," he added hopefully, "unless you want to ask the boys to chip in from their wages as you say your good-byes. I'll make up the difference when I get to town. They know I'm good for it."

Slocum let out a measured breath. When he pulled another one in to replace it, he got another taste of the expensive cheroot. The tobacco was good as ever, but did little to brighten his spirits. "You want me to go around begging for money I earned?"

"Begging is a harsh word."

"You owe me the money," Slocum said. "You'll pay up."

"I still need to go to town. Most of my funds are in the bank."

"You don't keep any here?"

"Like I already told you . . . I had wages to pay." Studying the cold scowl that was taking root on Slocum's face, Hal asked, "You ain't gonna try to rob me, are you?"

"No, but I ought to knock a few of your teeth out for asking that question."

"Take it easy, Slocum. It's been a rough day and it sounds like you've been through a hell of a lot. Let's not start fighting each other over something like money. You'll get yours. I got no reason to hold out." There was a knock on his office door, so Hal barked for whoever it was to come inside.

Robbie pushed the door open, saw Slocum, and gave him a friendly nod. Once he saw the fire in Slocum's eyes, however, the ranch hand quickly got back to the business at hand. "Some of your stolen cattle are back," he said to Hal.

"They just wander in on their own?" Hal asked.

"No, sir," Robbie replied. "Mr. Slocum brought them in. Along with some that . . . uhh . . . well . . . along with some that have Mr. Landry's brand."

"Is there enough to replace what I lost?"

"Not quite, but it's a start."

"Yes," Hal said proudly as he nodded toward Slocum. "It sure is. Thanks, Robbie. Do me a favor and keep Landry's stock separate from my own."

"Don't want to spread the curse around?" Slocum asked.

"No," Hal replied simply. "I sure wouldn't want to do that."

Hal and Robbie discussed a few other matters of ranch business, which gave Slocum a bit of time to simmer down. Now that he looked back on the events of the day, he supposed there wasn't too much to be upset about. Even when he'd been surrounded by armed men, Slocum hadn't had any trouble getting away, and he'd even gotten a measure of payback to boot. The stock he'd taken wasn't much, but it did feel awfully good to thumb his nose in Landry's direction before putting that spread behind him.

As for his business at the Singer Moon, Slocum had no doubt he'd get the money he was owed. Hal Singer might have been plenty of things, but he still didn't strike Slocum as the sort to back out on paying a man his agreed wages.

If there were to be repercussions for what happened at the Landry place, Slocum would deal with them. In fact, he'd be more than happy to discuss the matter with the rancher or any of the asshole gunmen he decided to hire.

For the moment, things had gone fairly well, and Slocum had done enough to make up for allowing those cattle to be stolen in the first place. Now that he'd gotten most of the animals back, as well as a confession from the man who'd paid to have them stolen, Slocum figured his end had been held up just fine. All that remained was to collect his earnings and be on his way. He was definitely looking forward to both.

"How's that sound to you, Slocum?" Hal asked.

Shaking himself from his own thoughts, Slocum replied, "What was that? I wasn't paying attention."

"There's a matter to be handled in town that requires my attention," Hal said. "Since I'm headed that way, I figured I could stop by the bank and get your money. How's that sound to you?"

"Sounds just fine," Slocum replied. "I'll come with you. We can take those rustlers in to Sheriff Bilson while we're there."

"Even better, we can stop by Landry's place along the way. Robbie, gather up five or six of the others to come along. Tell 'em to load for bear."

"Hold on a second," Slocum said before Hal could get too excited. "I didn't agree to that."

"Why not? You said yourself that those men weren't killers. Since you already got the shooting started, I just thought—"

"You took a shot at Landry?" Robbie asked.

"No," Slocum said to the ranch hand. Shifting his eyes toward Hal, he added, "And no, I won't be put to work as hired muscle for you, Hal."

"You know I can pay," the rancher pointed out.

"Yeah, but—"

"Then will you at least come along with me and my boys to the Landry place? All I want to do is collect my cattle and be on my way. I'll even take back the head you rode off with as a measure of good faith."

"And what if someone shoots their mouth off?" Slocum asked.

"Landry shooting his mouth off ain't news to anyone. After all this time sharing a fence line with the son of a bitch, I know how to ignore the hot air that he spews."

Just when Slocum wanted to refuse the request and demand his money, he was struck by the same feeling that had gotten him to go to the Landry ranch in the first place. It was a feeling that was like a small boot kicking him in the gut and staying there: not exactly guilt, but something that came a bit too close for Slocum's taste. If it had just been Hal, Slocum could have washed the feeling away with a glass of whiskey and gone happily about his business. But now it looked like Robbie was also going to have to march in and deal with Landry. Robbie and the other hands at the Singer Moon were good men. They were honest workers, and relied too much on Hal's wages to tell him to stuff orders that might be too dangerous to carry out. What galled Slocum the most was that there wouldn't have been any danger to speak of if he himself hadn't gotten it rolling.

"Fine," Slocum said. "I'll go." Just as Hal's face brightened, Slocum added, "But I won't be a party to any more of this bullshit between you and Landry. We're there to get the livestock and go. Save the rest for some other day."

Hal raised his arms again. This time, however, the grin that formed around the cheroot wedged between his teeth made him look more like the robber than someone being held up. "That's all I intended, Slocum. You think I want to get my men hurt?"

Since answering that question honestly would only prolong the conversation, Slocum let it rest. "When do we head out?" he asked.

"As soon as I can get everything together. Robbie, how long will it take to collect Landry's cows?"

The ranch hand shrugged. "Not long, I suppose. They're probably still where we left 'em."

"Good. Get them, those rustlers, and the boys ready for the trip. Make sure they're heeled, but tell them not to start anything or I'll have their asses hanging from the side of my barn." Glancing at Slocum, Hal asked, "Sound good enough?"

Slocum's only reply was a heavy sigh before he turned and walked from the office.

6

Since most of the ranch hands that had helped round up the cattle Slocum had brought back were still nearby, it hadn't taken much to get them moving again. Robbie led the hands back in the same direction from which they'd come to round up the cattle, while explaining what was in store for the rest of the day. Slocum watched the younger men go while leaning against the side of the bunkhouse. There was still a bit of his cheroot to smoke, so he decided to enjoy it while there was a moment of peace to do so.

"What are you doing back here, John?" Kelly asked as she walked over to stand beside him.

Taking the cheroot from his mouth, Slocum replied, "Enjoying the quiet. At least, I was."

"Forget I said anything."

The edge in Kelly's tone snapped Slocum out of his foul mood. The way she'd allowed the front of her blouse to come open just enough to display a good amount of cleavage didn't hurt either. Reaching out to grab her hip, Slocum pulled her back. She hadn't been trying too hard to get away, so she quickly found herself bumping against him.

"What do you want?" she snapped. "You want to be alone? I'll go. You want to leave so badly, then just go."

Slocum slipped his hand along her hip and then moved it around to hold her close. The longer he held her there, the more Kelly squirmed and looked around anxiously.

When she spoke again, the anger in her voice was replaced by barely contained excitement. "What's gotten into you?"

"I didn't mean to be an ass."

"All right, fine. Let me go."

"You really want that?" Slocum asked. "Or would you rather I pulled that skirt up around your waist and bent you over right here and now?"

Kelly pulled away from him in earnest this time. Once she was free, she looked at him with wide eyes. Her face was flushed and she was breathing twice as heavily as she'd been a few moments ago. "That's a wicked thing to say, John Slocum," she told him, even though her eyes were begging him to follow through on his promise.

"Maybe," Slocum said with a tired grin. "Maybe not."

Although she'd taken a few steps away, Kelly swung back around to stand in front of him. After a few moments, she stood on her tiptoes and leaned forward as if daring Slocum to grab her again. When he didn't, she lowered herself back down and leaned against the wall beside him.

"I hear there was some commotion over at the Landry place," she said.

"Yeah, you could say that."

"And now my uncle's getting a bunch of the boys together to head back out again. Are you going with them?"

Slocum looked over at her in disbelief. "What've you been doing? Listening in on every conversation that's held around here?"

"No," Kelly replied. She then fixed her eyes on another spot and held them there.

When Slocum turned to see what she was looking at, he found a cluster of the ranch hands circling around one another, strutting and twirling their guns as if they were putting on a show. Before long, Slocum could see Hal Singer among them displaying a fancy Sharps rifle.

"So," Kelly asked, "are you going with them?"

"Yep."

"Looks to me like they're all worked up to use those guns."

Slocum just chewed on his cheroot as the ember burned down to a nub.

"It's probably because of what you did," she pointed out. "There's talk that you went in there and laid down the law to Landry. That's something my uncle and just about everyone else in this place has wanted to do."

Slocum grunted under his breath as he took another puff.

"Even if you didn't go in shooting," Kelly went on to say, "you could stand to make a whole lot of money."

Shifting his gaze to her, Slocum asked, "How do you figure?"

"My uncle's willing to try anything if it'll bring Landry down a notch or two. I know for a fact that he's willing to pay for the privilege."

Slocum knew that as well. Even more, he knew Hal Singer was willing to hand money off to a woman claiming to be a witch just as long as she aimed her curses in the proper direction. "Where does all this between Hal and Landry come from?"

Kelly shrugged. "It was already started when I came to live here a few years ago. I always just thought it was some old argument that got out of hand and never died down. It seems both of those old men just got used to hating each other for whatever reason."

"Does it ever get bloody?"

"No. Sometimes the hired hands from each ranch get into a fight when they're in town at the same time. Every so often, my uncle steals some of Landry's business or Landry messes with the fence line, but it doesn't go much further than that. I've lived on other ranches and have seen things get a whole lot worse between neighbors."

Slocum could vouch for that. "What do you know about witches?" he asked.

Kelly chuckled once, which was the first reaction he'd gotten on the subject that made any sense. "The only witch I ever heard of was the one in Westlake."

And just like that, Slocum felt like the only person in the county with an ounce of common sense. After one more puff on his cheroot, Slocum could feel heat from the embers burning close to his face. He pinched the smoldering remains between his thumb and forefinger and then flicked it to the ground. Stomping out the cheroot under his heel, he said, "I suppose I'll get those rustlers loaded up and ready to go."

"Will you come back to meet me tonight?"

"If the witch doesn't get to me first."

Slocum led the drive to the Landry spread with something of an army behind him. Instead of soldiers, he had Hal Singer and a bunch of overly eager cowboys armed with any firearm they could find. And instead of cannons, he had a small herd of cattle covering the same ground they'd covered not too long ago, now trailing behind a pair of scowling thieves wrapped up tighter than a gift on Christmas morning.

Instead of trying to get from one point to another in as quick a time as possible, Slocum kept his pace slower and more deliberate so he could pick out any possible ambushes along the way. He was still convinced that Landry's hired hands weren't cold-blooded killers, but that didn't mean he was about to give them a chance to prove themselves otherwise.

Even with Slocum's precautions, the entire group made it to Landry's front gate in a reasonable amount of time. Slocum signaled for them to come to a stop, and that signal was passed on down the line. The only one to disobey the signal was the man riding a picturesque, coal black gelding. Hal Singer snapped his reins and raced his expensive horse up to Slocum.

"What's the matter?" Hal asked. "You see something?"

"Yeah," Slocum replied. "I see the front gate and I don't want to charge in like we're taking over the place."

"Aw, to hell with that. Landry stole from me and that's all there is to it. He should feel lucky we're comin' back at all." With that, Hal motioned frantically for the group to get moving again.

Robbie was the closest one to Slocum and Hal, so he was the one meant to pass the signal along. Before he did so, he waited to see what Slocum had in mind. Once he got the reluctant wave from him, Robbie let the others know they were moving on.

Assuming his men would follow his lead no matter where it took them, Hal raced toward the gate marking the front perimeter of Landry's property. Slocum followed him closely, preparing for whatever nonsense the rancher intended on pulling next.

Unlike the last time Slocum had been there, only one man greeted them at the gate. He was one of the younger hands who Slocum recognized from his earlier confrontation. Apparently, the younger man's memory was working just fine, because he winced and reached for his rifle boot the moment he got a look at who was headed his way.

"Not another step!" the young rifleman announced.

Slocum rode forward, positioned his horse between Hal and the gate, and then pulled back hard on his reins. Extending one arm back to Hal, Slocum looked ahead to the rifleman and said, "We're not here for any trouble. We just came to bring back Landry's cattle."

"And," Hal barked as he came to a stop at Slocum's side, "to get what's rightfully mine."

"You can send those cows on through," the rifleman

said. "Mr. Landry's already taken the rest of Mr. Singer's animals to be returned."

Despite all the talk Hal had done during the ride and all the intensity that was etched on his face at the moment, all he could think to say was, "Huh?"

The rifleman nodded so his cheek brushed against the stock of his weapon. "He left just over an hour ago."

Hal stood up in his stirrups and craned his neck in all directions. "We didn't see anyone headed our way," he said. "Did you see Landry and my cows, Slocum?"

Slocum didn't need to look around in order to answer that question. "No," he said. "I didn't see anyone."

"That's because they weren't headed for your property, Mr. Singer," the rifleman said. "They went into Westlake."

Hal dropped back down into his saddle with a thump. "That's a load of shit. Why the hell would he gather up all them animals just to take them into town?" Suddenly, Hal's face dropped. "He's gonna sell them, ain't he? That son of a bitch means to sell off *my* stock?"

"No," the rifleman quickly said. "He's gonna put them into safe hands so he can get things mediated."

"Mediated?"

"That's right. Mediated by Sheriff Bilson."

Slocum rolled his eyes. If there was anything he'd wanted to avoid, it was the involvement of some lawman who'd probably already been paid off by one or both of the ranchers. He would have preferred dragging some snake oil salesman or lawyer into the mix. At least that kind of scum was easier to work with.

Hal, on the other hand, didn't seem as upset by the prospect. After settling into his saddle, he nodded and finally said, "All right then. Maybe we'll just take all these cows into Westlake to see what the mediations come up with. Since I'm also bringing the assholes Landry hired to trim my herd, Bilson should see things my way."

"No," Slocum said. "These animals belong here, so they'll stay here."

Hal's eyes flashed with an angry fire. "That only puts Landry ahead of the game, Slocum!"

"This ain't no game. Besides, I shouldn't have taken the damn things anyway. Showing up with a piece of Landry's herd will just give him more kindling to add to the fire."

"Maybe, but—"

"If you want to drive them all the way to Westlake," Slocum interrupted, "then you can do it yourself."

Instead of riding off in a huff, all Slocum had to do was fix a glare onto Hal. The rancher backed down quick enough, but did so in a way that made it look like it was his own idea.

"We've dragged these tired heifers around too long already," Hal announced. "Go on, boys! Show 'em to the fence and be done with it."

Both Hal and Slocum watched as the ranch hands herded the cows back onto Landry's property. Throughout the entire process, the rifleman on the other side of that fence watched Slocum without once letting his rifle drop from his shoulder. The handoff didn't take long, and soon Hal's men were lined up outside Landry's gate.

"Much obliged," the rifleman said as if he was expecting a double cross at any second.

Slocum tipped his hat. "Sorry about the confusion earlier."

Gritting his teeth to make it clear he hadn't forgotten about the stout man who'd been killed, the rifleman said, "You'll answer for that, mister. Don't worry none about that."

"This was a civil exchange," Slocum replied. "Don't ruin it now."

"Yeah," Robbie added as he rode up to stop beside Slocum, "especially when you're so outnumbered."

The rifleman stared at all the other men over his barrel,

and then shot a quick glance over his shoulder. The cattle were already finding spots to graze and there was still nobody else coming to his aid. The fact that the rifleman even looked for help was enough to tell Slocum that there were likely more of Landry's men kicking around somewhere not too far away.

"Our business is done here," Hal announced. "Let's get to town before it gets too late." With that, Hal pointed his horse's nose in the direction of Westlake and snapped his reins.

One by one, Hal's ranch hands turned away from the gate to follow their boss. Finally, Slocum, Robbie, and the trussed-up rustlers were the only ones left. When Robbie started to back away, Slocum watched the rifleman's face. Although still anxious, the young man on the other side of the fence didn't look ready to pull his trigger.

"Go on, Robbie," Slocum said. "I'm right with you."

Leading the prisoners' horses by the reins, Robbie raced to catch up to the rest of the group.

It went against the grain for Slocum to turn his back to an armed man. That was only giving a coward the chance to do the most damage possible. Then again, the only other way to make things better was to put the rifleman down before leaving that gate. Since the man probably wouldn't respond to a cordial request, that left Slocum with one very messy option.

Rather than draw his Colt and put that option into effect, Slocum pulled back on his reins until his horse retreated from the fence. All the while, Slocum watched the rifleman's face for any hint that the young man might try something stupid. As with the first time he'd squared off against Landry's men, Slocum didn't see the eyes of a killer looking back at him.

There was plenty of nervousness and fear, which Slocum knew was in his favor as he put some more distance between himself and that rifle. The farther away Slocum got, the harder it would be for the man to fire an accurate shot. And, considering how rattled the younger man looked, Slocum guessed his odds were pretty good even at close range.

Once he'd put his chances at well above average, Slocum steered his horse toward Hal and the others and tapped his heels against its sides. His hand remained close to his pistol, but the rifleman never fired a shot.

7

Westlake was a good-sized cow town, but far from the biggest Slocum had ever seen. Like any other cow town, its main streets were wide-open to accommodate wagons of all sizes and arranged to funnel incoming riders toward rows of saloons and whorehouses that had been built to deprive customers of their money. There were plenty of stables and corrals on the perimeter, along with fenced-in plots of land meant for small groups of large animals awaiting sale or inspection. At the moment, most of the corrals were full.

Hal Singer rushed ahead of the group to get a closer look at the cattle milling about inside one of those fenced-in sections. It didn't take him long to spot the circles and lines that made up his ranch's brand. "Those are from my herd!" he announced.

Slocum and Robbie both approached the large pen and took a gander for themselves. "Yep," Slocum replied. "Looks that way."

"Well, don't just stand there gawking!" Hal said. "Get them out of there and let's drive them back to where they belong."

"You'll do no such thing!"

Until that moment, Hal obviously hadn't seen the man within the small shed built next to the corral. He snapped his head toward that shack as if it and the rest of the town had simply sprouted up from the dirt. "Don't tell me what to do with my own property, Nate," Hal said. "These are mine and I'm taking them back."

Nate was a fellow in his mid-twenties who carried himself with an easy confidence. He held his chin up and his back straight due, in no small part, to the gun he wore and the badge pinned to his shirt. Keeping one hand on the grip of his holstered six-shooter, Nate extended his other arm to shoo the men away from the corral. "I know whose cows these are," he said. "We ain't blind. The sheriff just wants them held here for now."

"What for?"

"On account of the mediation, that's what for."

Rolling his eyes, Hal grumbled, "Oh, for Christ's sake."

"Go see Sheriff Bilson. He'll explain it to you."

"All I want is my damn cattle. And where are the horses?" Hal asked. "I'm short a couple of those as well, you know!"

"Tell it to the sheriff."

Grinding his teeth together, Hal nodded stiffly and then turned toward the men that had followed him this far. "We're gonna go see the sheriff," he announced as if that had been his intention all along.

Slocum and Robbie followed behind Hal, who paraded down the streets of Westlake like he'd conquered the place. The remaining ranch hands were too busy deciding which saloon to hit first and gawking at the ladies to worry about much else. By the time they reached the sheriff's office, everyone in the group was looking in a different direction.

"You two," Hal said as he motioned toward some of the ranch hands that were lagging behind. "Go see what the hell those boys are doing."

The pair that Hal had addressed snapped to attention and rode up alongside their boss. Neither one of them was out of their teens and they hadn't stopped fidgeting since they'd crossed into the town's limits. "What boys, Mr. Singer?" the older of the two asked.

Hal kept his finger pointing toward a nearby saloon and said, "Them boys outside that saloon. They work for Landry. Go see what the hell they're doing here."

"If you want to talk to the sheriff, just go talk to him," Slocum said. "No need to stir anything else up."

"Good point, Slocum," Hal said with a curt nod. "I'll go talk to the sheriff and you go see what those boys are doing."

"Who the hell cares what they're doing?"

"Maybe they know what Landry's got up his sleeve with this mediation business. I'm the one paying all of your salaries, so you'll do as I ask, damn it!"

Slocum didn't put up any more fuss. He simply nodded and replied, "You're right. Go have your talk. It sounds like Landry is probably with the sheriff as well."

Hal blinked in surprise a few times before puffing out his chest. "I believe he may just be there and I believe I will have that talk. Come find me when you learn something."

Nodding once to Hal, Slocum waited for the rancher to dismount and strut away. He only had to wait a few seconds before Hal had gathered so much steam in his stride that a brick wall couldn't have stopped him.

"Shouldn't one of us go with him?" Robbie asked.

Slocum shrugged and rode toward the saloon. "Why? Shouldn't he be safe with the sheriff?"

"Yeah, but if Landry is there . . ."

"Then both of them can give the sheriff a headache instead of me. I need a drink. You coming?"

Since Hal was charging away and Slocum didn't seem concerned enough to stop him, Robbie decided to follow the rest of the men toward the saloon.

Slocum rode straight toward the Bull's Horn Saloon with a good portion of Hal Singer's employees backing him up. That was probably why he attracted so much attention from the other cowboys that were already standing in front of the place. Slocum recognized a few of those men as ones that had pointed guns at him back at the Landry place. Their guns were holstered at the moment, however, which meant none of them were eager to be the first to get in Slocum's way.

"Don't piss your trousers, boy," Slocum said as he dismounted and walked right past one of the younger men in the bunch. "We're just here for a drink." With that, he pushed open the saloon's front door and walked inside.

Both sets of ranch hands bristled as Singer's men walked past Landry's. There were a few unkind words traded between them, but nothing more than that. Slocum figured if he could make it into the saloon without sparking a fight, he was in the clear. For the moment, it seemed he was right.

Slocum walked up to the bar, fully expecting to hear knuckles cracking against someone's jaw or a skull being smashed into a wall. All he got was the steady flow of noise that filled any other saloon. For Slocum, that was better than music.

"What can I get for ya?" the bartender asked.

"Whiskey. Make it a bottle. In fact, make it two."

After letting out a slow whistle, the barkeep asked, "You looking to drown some sorrows, mister?"

"Only one's for me." Waving toward Robbie and the other hands, Slocum added, "Let these fellas fight for the other one."

Robbie sidled up to the bar and said, "A few glasses will be just fine."

True to his word, Slocum took hold of the first bottle by the neck, poured himself a glass, and maintained his grip on it. "Suit yourself." He tossed back that first drink and then let out a slow sigh. The whiskey burned all the way down his throat like a warm fire that untied all the knots that had been cinching into his innards. As good as that first drink was, the second was even better.

Suddenly, Slocum spotted an answer to a problem that had been nagging at him since he'd first caught sight of the hands from the Landry place. As well intentioned as he knew Robbie and the others to be, Slocum knew one of them would throw a punch sooner or later, or be provoked into doing so by one of Landry's men. Trouble was brewing, and it wouldn't take long for the storm to hit. Of course, Slocum didn't intend on just sitting and waiting for it.

The Bull's Horn was a modest saloon, but a busy one. Drunks leaned against a bar that looked to be cobbled together from crates, old shelves, and anything else that was sturdy enough to support some weight. Tables of all sizes were scattered throughout the place, surrounded by chairs that seemed to have been pulled in from a dozen different sources. Pictures in broken frames adorned the walls. The mirror hanging behind the bar was so cracked and filthy that it no longer cast a reflection. The only reason the damn thing had probably been left up there was because it was too much of a bother to take down.

Slocum took another drink straight from his bottle before collecting a few glasses and walking toward the other end of the bar.

"Where you headed, Slocum?" Robbie asked.

"Don't worry about that. Just make sure everyone's glass stays full. Keep an eye on the door, too."

"You want me to keep Landry's boys out of here?"

"No. Just keep our men from starting any trouble."

Robbie winced as he looked between the front door and the group of hands from Hal's ranch. When he leaned over to Slocum, he said, "I may not be able to keep things quiet for very long."

"Don't fret it," Slocum replied as he resumed walking along the bar.

Slocum didn't need to see Robbie's face to imagine the expression on it. However, he'd worked with the ranch hand long enough to trust him to follow through on what he'd been told. As long as there was free whiskey to be poured, Robbie would do it.

Slocum knew the others were in capable hands as he approached the person at the end of the bar who had caught his attention. Since the dark-haired woman wasn't doing much to conceal the generous curves beneath her partially buttoned blouse, Slocum guessed she'd caught plenty of men's attention. In fact, it was most likely her job to do that very thing. There was another man talking to the woman, so Slocum waited his turn. Even from where he stood, however, he could smell the reek of liquor-drenched breath emanating from the filthy man.

"Tha's an outgregious . . . an outstand . . . a . . ." The drunk stopped stammering long enough to pull in a haggard breath and then say, "An outrageous price! Tha's what it is! Outrageous!"

The woman's hair was long and tousled. Her cream-colored blouse was tucked into a black and red skirt that she'd hiked up just enough to display the leg that was propped on the bottom bar rail. Her face was prettier than the other women's faces in the Bull's Horn, and her body was simply outstanding. Running her hands along the sides of her large breasts, she asked, "Don't you think all this is worth that much?"

Even though the drunk was trying to maintain a strong facade, his efforts broke down the moment he let his eyes wander along the woman's body. Her hands lingered just long enough to draw attention to the outline of her nipples pressing against her blouse. Swallowing hard, the drunk meekly replied, "I jus' don't got that much."

"Well, then," she told him as she took her hands away, "you won't get me either."

The drunk straightened up and squared his shoulders. "You can't do that! I talked all . . . I came here and . . ."

"Look, why don't you go over to one of the other girls? There's plenty to choose from."

"I don' want them. I want you! And I'll have you!" Just as the drunk reached out for the prizes he'd been staring at for most of the conversation, a hand dropped on his shoulder like a hammer and spun him around. Once his vision cleared, the drunk was looking at a very different chest indeed.

"That'll be enough, old-timer," Slocum said. "If you don't have the money, you gotta step aside."

Lifting his eyes up to meet Slocum's, the drunk stared at him for a few seconds while more putrid breath slowly rolled out of his mouth. His face had more wrinkles than a raisin, which probably made him look a lot older than he truly was. There could have been even more wrinkles in his neck and face, but there was too much dirt caked onto him for an accurate estimation.

"Why don' you min' yer own business?" the drunk slurred.

Just then, Slocum noticed the tin cup in the old man's hand. The drunk had such a grip on it that it was hard to say where his fingers ended and the cup began. "Here you go," Slocum said as he grabbed the drunk's wrist and poured a bit of whiskey into the tin cup. "That's for being a gentleman."

The drunk looked down at the cup and grinned. Once he lifted it to his nose to sniff at the cup's contents, his grin grew even wider. "Much obliged." Turning to the dark-haired woman, he fumbled his way through a wink and said, "I'll talk to you later, Lucille."

"See you around, sweetie." Once the drunk had staggered away, she turned toward Slocum. Looking him up and down, she asked, "What did I do to catch the eye of a man like you?"

"Just standing there seems to be enough to catch anyone's eye," Slocum replied. "So you're Lucille?"

"That's right." She extended her hand and asked, "What about you?"

"John Slocum. Pleased to meet you."

Lucille chuckled from the back of her throat as Slocum wrapped his hand around hers and shook it gently. "You're one of the men from the Singer Moon, aren't you?"

"That's right."

"I've had a few of those boys come pay me a visit. Why haven't you introduced yourself before now?"

"There's more than enough work to keep me busy." Also, thanks to Hal's niece, Slocum had had his fill of warm nights in a woman's embrace without needing to pay for the pleasure.

"At least you're rectifying that now. Thanks for the assistance, by the way. I'd hate to have that poor old fool tossed out on his ear again."

"Again?"

"Yeah, he takes a run at me a few times a week. As much as he drinks, he's probably forgotten what happened when he stepped out of line all them other times. I'd like to show you some appreciation," she told him as she slid her fingers down Slocum's chest. "And I sure wouldn't charge you as much as I was asking from ol' Skunk Breath."

"What about for them?" Slocum asked as he nodded toward the front door.

Lucille looked toward the front of the saloon, but kept her hand on Slocum. In fact, she slowly eased her hand down over his belt. "You mean your partners from the Singer Moon?"

"Not them. The ones standing outside."

The front door was either stuck or being propped open, because it hadn't shut all the way since Slocum had stepped through it. Landry's hired hands could be seen milling about outside, and a few of them were starting to find their way in.

"Oh," Lucille said. "Those are Landry's boys."

"That's right. I've got reason to believe they've got money burning holes in their pockets and they'd love to spend it on you and your friends."

Sliding her hand a bit lower, Lucille asked, "You know that for certain, do you?"

"Well, they're not dead and they're not blind. That means they must have a soft spot for a woman like yourself."

"Not too soft, I hope," Lucille whispered as she reached between Slocum's legs to massage him. It was only a matter of seconds before she grinned and said, "Not too soft at all. You sure you don't want to take the first run at me? I can steer some other girls toward those cowboys and take care of you special. I guarantee it'll be worth it."

"I don't doubt that for a minute," Slocum replied before he had a change of heart. "Right now, I need to keep those Landry boys occupied and if they don't get distracted by you and your girls, they'll kick up a storm that might put a kink in tonight's business."

Hearing that, Lucille looked over toward the front of the bar again. This time, she studied the place with sharp eyes that seemed to take in everything around her. "I suppose I shouldn't expect anything less than a fight when the Landry and Singer boys get together. You say they just got paid?"

"Probably not too long ago. I'm sure you girls know plenty of ways to get to the bottom of a man's pockets."

"Sure, but I'd rather just reach down and get a feel for myself," Lucille said as she did just that and cupped Slocum's groin until he strained even harder against his jeans. "Promise you'll come see me soon?"

"Most definitely."

Lucille nodded and took her hand away. "You better deliver, mister." With that, she turned her back to Slocum so she could cross the room to where a bunch of working girls had clustered together. She also gave Slocum a lingering view of her backside as she swayed invitingly beneath her skirt.

In no time at all, Lucille had rounded up no fewer than five other girls from every corner of the saloon. They moved like a pack of wolves to the front of the place and by the time they got there, most folks in the saloon thought the women were putting on a show. When the hands from the Landry place saw they were the ones in the ladies' sights, they barely knew what to do.

Slocum walked over to stand with Robbie and the others from Hal's ranch. All of them were staring at the spectacle being created by the working girls.

"How the hell did those assholes get so lucky?" one of the cowboys asked.

Extending his arm to fill the man's glass, Slocum replied, "Why don't we try our luck somewhere else?"

Robbie pulled his eyes away from the closest working girl, who was bending over to show her wares to one of Landry's men. Even from the back end, the view was just fine. "Aren't we supposed to find out what those men are up to?"

"I can see what they're up to from here," Slocum said. "And I can tell you what they'll be doing before too long. That don't mean I want to stand around and watch."

Robbie grinned. "I suppose you're right. Hal probably just meant for us to keep 'em occupied. This way, we don't have to get our noses bloodied."

Slocum, Robbie, and the rest of Hal's men walked out of the saloon right past Landry's boys. Even though the men from the other ranch saw them leaving, the working girls were doing plenty to keep them from following. A couple of Landry's men were already being led to one of the saloon's back rooms, while the others were enjoying the women's colorful negotiating process. Some of the women were rubbing the men's shoulders or rubbing themselves, but it was safe to say that none of Landry's men would voluntarily leave that saloon anytime soon.

Slocum led Hal's men away from the Bull's Horn and down the street. "There's plenty of places to choose from," he said. "Where should we go?"

Some of the men shouted out their suggestions, but

Slocum didn't care what the decision was. As long as they picked a spot away from all those Landry men, it was fine by him. There had already been one man from that ranch killed, and it would only make things complicated if he had a hand in hurting any more.

"At least tell me one thing," Robbie said.

"What's that?"

"Tell me you didn't pay for those women to hang all over those assholes like that."

"I didn't have to pay them a thing," Slocum replied. "I just gave them the scent, is all."

"Good, because I'd hate for—".

The rest of what Robbie said was swallowed up by a sudden rush of sound that filled Slocum's head like water. A dull thump sounded from somewhere, but Slocum could barely hear much more than a distant hint of it. Slowly, he realized he was falling, and before he could do anything about it, he was off his feet. Pain seeped in through the back of his skull, but Slocum didn't feel much of it before he was unconscious.

8

Slocum didn't even realize he'd passed out until well after he woke up again. The sounds rushing through his head made him feel as if he was being held under a rapidly flowing river. When he tried to move, he could only feel cold, slippery surfaces against all his extremities.

After taking a few more breaths, he realized he was flailing against a dirt floor and all the slipping was due to his weakened arms and legs. As the world rushed back to him, he regained some more control, and was finally able to lift himself up. Letting his head hang down, Slocum propped himself onto his hands and knees and filled his lungs a few more times.

Every breath Slocum took was more painful than the last. The effort of trying to open his eyes caused so much pain that he thought they might have been sewn shut. Slocum placed his hand on the back of his head to find a messy patch of blood encrusted in his hair. The knot under all that blood was almost as big as an apple. When he felt something touch his shoulder, he took a swing at it before it could get any closer.

"Take it easy, Slocum," a familiar voice said from somewhere nearby. "I only meant to help you up."

Slocum forced his eyes open. The room was dark, but he could just make out the face that matched the voice. "That you, Mack?"

"Yep."

Mack was another one of Hal's hands. In the time Slocum had worked at the Singer Moon, Mack had possibly spoken to him twice. Since Mack tended to keep to himself no matter who was trying to talk to him, Slocum never took offense. Mack was a hard worker who didn't kick up any dust, so Slocum hadn't worried about him back at the Bull's Horn.

"What the hell happened?" Slocum asked. "Did one of those Landry men bushwhack me?"

"You got bushwhacked all right," Mack replied. "But not by any of Landry's men. Sheriff Bilson had that honor. Or maybe it was one of his deputies."

"A deputy? What?" With Mack's help, Slocum was able to get to his feet. He took another look around, but wasn't able to see much. The room was small and dark, but seemed to be open because there was some light streaming in from a nearby doorway. As Slocum tried to walk toward that door to get a look outside, he was stopped by Mack.

"You don't wanna do that," Mack warned.

"Why not?"

"Because you ain't slim enough to fit between those bars."

Slocum concentrated on focusing his eyes. Although his head was still filled with a dull roar, he was soon able to make out the iron bars covering the opening in the door. Slocum stepped forward to grab two of those bars and press his face against them to see whatever he could. The main door of the little jailhouse faced the street, and plenty of sounds drifted in from the nearby saloon district. What struck him even more was just how dark the sky was.

"How long have I been in here?" Slocum asked.

"A bit longer than me," Mack replied. "So that'd be some hours. I don't have a watch to know for certain."

Rattling the bars, Slocum found there to be a bit of give in them, but not nearly enough for him to hope for escape. "So a deputy knocked me in the head and dumped me in here?"

Mack stepped up beside Slocum and looked through the bars. "I didn't see it, but Robbie said you were put down, and at first the rest of us figured Landry's men had some-thin' to do with it."

"I thought you were all coming with me to another sa-loon."

"A few of us lagged behind," Mack admitted. "Them ladies were puttin' on a hell of a show."

"All right, fine. Then what happened?"

"We was nearby, so we saw you on the ground," Mack continued. "There were some lawmen about when Landry's men rushed over to shoot off their mouths, and it all went to hell from there. Robbie tried to pull 'em apart, but me and some of the other boys heard some things we didn't like."

"And what might that have been?"

Mack smirked and said, "The sound of those assholes' voices."

Despite the clanging in his ears and the throbbing pain in his head, Slocum had to smile at that. He might'n have known Mack too well, but he was already starting to like him a bit more. "Did Robbie and the rest get away?"

"Nah," Mack replied as he made a fist and looked down to a set of knuckles that appeared to have been scraped against sandstone. "They just didn't split anyone's face open. The sheriff let them go with a warning, but I got tossed in here with you."

"What about the guy with the split face?"

"He won't be impressin' any ladies for a while, that's for certain."

Pulling in one more deep breath, Slocum turned away

from the bars. He'd never studied the jailhouse before, but it looked just like a shack. The single cell was the size of a small cabin's living space. A thick wall and the barred door sectioned the cell off from a small, closet-sized room that led outside. There were small windows on two of the walls that were hardly big enough to slip a hand through. The floor was made of weathered planks that were so old and tough, they might very well have been petrified. There was no furniture, no bunks, and no chamber pot. There was, however, a pair of other prisoners at the back of the room.

"Who are they?" Slocum asked.

Mack looked back there and shrugged. "Hell if I know. They were here when I got here. I think one of 'em's drunk. Either that or he's dead, because he ain't moved as far as I can tell."

Putting his back to the wall, Slocum lowered his head and leveled his eyes at the figures at the back of the room. Upon closer examination, he realized the drunk was the same old man that had been accosting Lucille back at the Bull's Horn. Apparently, he truly didn't know when to leave well enough alone. He was lying on his side and curled into a ball. The second figure sat with his back to the wall and his legs drawn up close to his body. His head was balanced a little too well upon his knees for him to be asleep.

Slocum had seen plenty worse jails before, but this one was solid enough to keep him inside for a while. If that was the case, he knew he had to show he wasn't some wounded animal that could barely stand on his own. Keeping his shoulders squared to the second figure, he asked, "Who's back there? You one of Landry's men?"

The man in the back remained quiet.

Watching the other two closely, Mack said, "I don't think he'll answer, but I don't think he'll be any trouble either. It ain't like this town's full of wanted men or anything. He's probably just another drunk or a troublemaker."

"Just like us," Slocum said.

Mack chuckled and dropped down to sit with his back to the wall adjacent to the door. "Yeah. Just like us."

Slocum grabbed the bars and rattled them some more. Something inside him wanted to keep shaking those bars until they gave way or he got tuckered out. That same something wanted to slam his shoulder against the door until it broke off its hinges. Choking down the anger that any caged animal felt, Slocum picked a spot against a wall that allowed him to watch the door as well as all the other prisoners. In the blind hope that the lawmen in Westlake were complete idiots, he checked his holster and his pockets.

His gun belt was gone and his pockets were empty.

"So how long am I supposed to be in here for?" Slocum asked.

"I didn't ask. Last time I saw any of them law dogs, I was getting tossed in here like a sack of potatoes," Mack said. "Robbie should be comin' for us, though. Either him or Hal."

For some reason, that didn't make Slocum feel any better.

A few hours passed. It was difficult for Slocum to judge just how long he sat in there because he kept nodding off. He could have slept for a few seconds, a few minutes, or possibly an hour at a stretch. All he knew was that all the prisoners inside the jailhouse remained rooted in their spots until the rattle of a key in a rusted lock broke the silence. Mack and Slocum jumped to their feet, but the two in the back of the cell stayed right where they were.

As the door swung open, the twin, blunt barrels of a shotgun poked through like a snake peeking into a rabbit's hole. "Everyone back away from the door or I'll burn you down," snarled the deputy behind the shotgun.

Slocum didn't step any closer, but he also didn't back away. "I want to see the sheriff," he said.

The deputy with the shotgun filled the narrow space

between the cell door and freedom. "You'll see him in the morning, asshole. Now step back."

Slocum had a hard time fighting his animal instinct even though he was looking at the wrong end of a shotgun. "Why the hell was I tossed in here? You can't just keep me prisoner for no good reason."

"No? Well, I can put you in the ground for tryin' to escape."

Reluctantly, Slocum took one step back and stopped. That was apparently enough for the deputy, because the door to the cell was pulled open. A group of three men were herded into the cell like sheep by the deputy with the shotgun and another lawman. Once the new prisoners were inside, the second deputy kicked the door shut and locked it.

The lawman with the shotgun peeked through the bars and said, "Sleep tight now."

Slocum rushed toward the door and grabbed the bars. He still wasn't able to pull the bars loose, but he got a real good look at the two lawmen laughing at him as they walked away. Turning around, Slocum studied the prisoners who had just been added to the group. Every one of them worked for Landry.

"Well, what have we here?" Slocum mused. "Seems that you boys got yourselves into some trouble."

Mack stepped up to stand beside Slocum. "These were the ones I told you about. The ones that started that scrap with Robbie and the others."

"We didn't start anything!" one of the three new arrivals snapped. "You pricks were the ones who started throwing punches."

The second Landry man had rough skin that hung down from his face like old leather. He was one of the better-known cowhands from that ranch on account of all the fights he was known to start. Everyone called him Coyote. Raising a hand to point at Slocum, Coyote snarled, "That one there is the fella who killed Paul."

"Was Paul the short, fat bastard who thought he could gun me down?" Slocum asked. "I do recall killing that one."

And that was all Slocum needed to say. Those words might as well have been the lit match touched to the end of a short fuse. Coyote and the other two Landry men rushed forward with their fists clenched and their eyes wide-open. Mack lowered his shoulder and stampeded directly into the closest man, while Slocum let out a howl and jumped into the fray.

After the day he'd had, it felt damn good for Slocum to get his hands dirty by confronting someone head-on. Being concerned about getting folks hurt or messing up a job or running afoul of the wrong people just didn't suit him. As soon as his fist cracked against Coyote's jaw, Slocum was reminded of why he preferred to work on his own. It was just plain simpler that way.

Coyote let out a grunt as Slocum knocked his head back with one punch. When Coyote looked up again, the ugly brawler was grinning. "You got more'n that, don't ya, boy?" With that, Coyote absorbed a punch to the stomach before burying his fist into Slocum's chest.

The impact of the punch made it difficult for Slocum to breathe, but he wasn't going to be slowed down just yet. Instead, he crumpled and staggered back a step to make Coyote feel good and strong. Just when the other man came at him for what he thought would be the finishing blow, Slocum lashed out with a powerful kick to Coyote's leg. Slocum must have still been feeling the effects of getting knocked in the head, because his aim fell just short of snapping Coyote's knee.

Coyote was still smiling, even as he hobbled to one side. "Oh, you done it now."

Slocum was smiling, too, as he replied, "Let's just see about that."

Both men threw themselves at each other amid a flurry of fists. When they met, the impact was akin to two stags locking horns.

Within a few feet of Slocum, Mack was squaring off with one of the other Landry men. The first one was still on the floor after taking the full brunt of Mack's original charge. His lip had been split and he groaned every time he tried to get up. That left Mack with only one opponent to worry about.

Mack took a swing at the man, which sliced through empty air. Before he could cock his arm back again, Landry's man punched him in the face. Mack's head snapped around with enough force to rattle his back teeth. Nodding to himself, Mack swung his left fist in a high arc. As soon as the other man ducked to avoid that punch, Mack dug in his heels and hooked his right hand in a vicious uppercut that pounded against the other man's stomach. When the cowboy folded over, he hurled the contents of his stomach onto the jailhouse floor.

Hearing that, Slocum looked over to see if Mack was in any trouble. The good news was that his partner was the one dishing out the pain instead of receiving it. The bad news was that Slocum had turned away just long enough for Coyote to gather his strength and deliver a quick punch to Slocum's kidneys.

"You like that?" Coyote snarled as he came up behind him and wrapped one arm around Slocum's throat. Remaining at Slocum's back, Coyote added, "What about this, huh?"

Even though he knew the follow-up punch was coming, there wasn't much Slocum could do to prevent it. The blow hit his ribs and sent a wave of agony throughout Slocum's entire body. He reached up to grab hold of the arm that encircled his throat, got a good grip, and then bent forward to take Coyote off his feet.

The bigger man yelped as he was tossed against a wall. After he landed in a heap, it took Coyote a few seconds to figure out which direction was up.

"How you doing, Mack?" Slocum asked.

Rubbing his fist, Mack replied, "I might'a cracked a knuckle or two, but I can't complain. What about you?"

"I'm havin' a hell of a time!" Slocum said as he rushed forward to drive his knee into Coyote's face.

Mack spotted some movement from the cowboy with the split lip, and rushed over to put him down before he could tip the odds in the Landry men's favor. Although he'd been the first one to drop, that man wasn't out of the picture just yet. He was pulling himself to his feet as his partner was trying to sneak up on Mack from another side.

Before he could put the first cowboy back on the floor, Mack saw some movement from the corner of his eye. He snapped his head and elbow around at the same time to crack the second cowboy in the head. That man staggered back half a step, but came back at Mack with renewed vigor. It was all Mack could do to grab hold of the cowboy before he was trampled.

As those two tussled, the cowboy with the split lip pulled himself up and took in the situation. Mack was closest to him, but he was throwing punches like a man possessed. Slocum, on the other hand, was dealing with Coyote while keeping his back to the rest of the room. Picking the easier of the two targets, he stalked over to try and get the drop on Slocum.

Coyote was taking a beating, but quickly turned the tide when he snapped a lucky mule kick into Slocum's leg. The kick didn't do a lot of damage, but it pushed Slocum back far enough to give Coyote some breathing room. The big, ugly brawler bared his teeth and took advantage of the opening he'd created by rushing at Slocum. Because Slocum was preparing for Coyote's attack, he wasn't ready for what the cowboy behind him had in store.

Clasping both hands together, the cowboy lifted his arms as if he was going to drive a stake into the ground with a hammer. Slocum still had his back to him, presenting a perfect target. Before he could deliver his blow, however, the

cowboy felt something tear at the bare skin of his neck.
Wheeling around, the cowboy found himself face-to-face
with a slender woman with wild eyes. The sight took him
off his guard long enough for the woman to lash out with
her right hand. Her nails scraped against the cowboy's face
in much the same way that she'd scratched his neck. This
time, however, she was able to dig them in a little deeper.

"What the hell?" the cowboy yelped.

Slocum sent a quick jab into Coyote's gnarled face, and
then rushed forward to grab hold of the cowboy with the
split lip and fresh scratches. Then Slocum lifted the cowboy
from his feet and tossed him toward Coyote. The blood was
coursing fast enough through Slocum's veins that he was
able to hit one man with the other. Even though he knew the
fight wasn't over, he stopped short when he saw the woman
standing there.

Mack was still wrestling with the remaining Landry
worker. Coyote and the other cowboy were piled on top of
each other, and the drunk still slept against the far wall.
That meant the figure who'd been sitting and staring at him
earlier hadn't been a lanky man after all.

The woman had dark skin and eyes that were drawn
into angry slits. Since she didn't make a move against him,
Slocum shifted his attention back to Coyote and the cowboy
that was heaped on top of him.

"Get the hell off me!" Coyote said as he threw the other
man toward Slocum.

Slocum was happy to add to the cowboy's fresh injuries
with a punch that started all the way down near his boots
and ended squarely on the other man's jaw. The cowboy
fell back toward Coyote, who caught him and then threw
him aside like an old newspaper.

"Come on, asshole," Slocum said as he waved Coyote
toward him. "Or are you content to keep playing with your
little friend?"

The taunt might have pushed Coyote over the edge, or the ugly fighter might have already been too mad to hear it. Either way, Coyote lowered his shoulder and charged at Slocum while letting out a howl that filled the entire room.

Slocum waited for the last second, and then stepped aside while pivoting on one foot. He was able to snag Coyote's shirt with one hand and his belt with the other. That way, Slocum could use Coyote's own momentum to launch him face-first toward the door.

Coyote tried to stop, but he was already moving too fast. The bars held, but were loose enough to move a bit on impact. Coyote's head hit the space between two of them, and didn't stop until his shoulders pounded against the iron rods. When he tried to pull back, Coyote realized his head was wedged firmly between the bars.

Mack had a handful of the remaining cowboy's hair, which he used to drop the man's head down as he snapped his knee up. The two met with a wet crunch and when Mack released his grip, the cowboy dropped into a heap on the floor. "What the hell did you do, Slocum?"

Slocum shook his head and took a long look at the sight in front of him. The more Coyote tried to pull his head free, the funnier it looked. "I think I just found someone who's got a worse headache than I do."

When Coyote started cursing and pounding his fists against the door, both Slocum and Mack were doubled over with laughter. The laughter stopped, however, when Slocum saw the glare in the eyes of the only Landry man that was still standing.

"You're dead," the cowboy said through the bloody mask created by his split lip and scratched face.

"Yeah?" Slocum asked. "How do you figure?"

"You killed Paul and you'll hang for it. All this fighting just proves you're a goddamned wild dog that should be put out of its misery."

Slocum walked forward to grab the cowboy by the front of his shirt. "If that's the case, then I might as well put you in some misery as well."

Slocum balled up his fist and took his time cocking it back. As he watched the cowboy wince in preparation for the punch, Slocum heard the familiar rattle of a key within the lock.

"What's with all the damned noise?" the deputy with the shotgun asked from the smaller of the two rooms. When he tried opening the cell door, he heard a pained howl from Coyote. The deputy looked down at the head that was wedged between the bars at knee level. "What in the hell is this?"

"Just get me outta here!" Coyote whined.

After a whole lot of wrangling, one of the deputies was able to get the door open while the other covered the prisoners with the shotgun. Coyote had to crawl on the ground to prevent the swinging door from slowly twisting his head off his shoulders.

Once the door was halfway open, the deputy with the shotgun pointed to the remaining two Landry men and said, "You two, get out and go home."

"What?" Slocum asked.

"They're just in here for brawling, so they're getting turned loose," the deputy replied. "You, too, Mack. Get out of here."

Mack looked over at Slocum, who nodded once for him to go. After Mack was outside, Slocum asked, "What about the rest of us?"

"Soon as that drunk wakes up, he'll be booted out. You're not goin' anywhere just yet. Leastways, you won't be goin' far."

"Why?"

"Because you killed a man," the deputy snarled. "That's a far cry from throwing a few punches in front of a saloon. And don't try to whine about it, because the sheriff's got plenty of witnesses that saw what you did."

Slocum glared back at the lawman, but couldn't dispute the claim. He'd expected to answer for shooting Landry's gunman, but he'd hoped to do it more on his own terms. "And what about her?" Slocum asked.

The deputy glanced at the slender woman who stood her ground toward the back of the room and said, "You kill that witch and you're free as a bird. That offer comes straight from Sheriff Bilson."

"And he can shove it straight up his ass," Slocum replied.

"Then you can spend the night in the box."

9

The box turned out to be another old shack that had been converted for use as a jail. Unlike the previous jailhouse, this one was barely larger than an outhouse, and only had one window that was several inches above eye level. Slocum was led to the box at the end of the deputy's shotgun and shoved inside by a boot to his back. Just as Slocum turned around, he'd been forced to catch the dark-skinned woman as she was tossed in after him.

"When's my trial?" Slocum shouted.

The deputy responded by telling him, "Don't need a trial. Mr. Landry says you're a killer and killers get hung at first light." After what sounded like three locks were fixed into place, the lawmen stomped away.

Slocum looked down at the woman in his arms. "So," he said. "You're the witch of Westlake?"

She pulled away from him, but could barely take two steps before hitting the wall. Turning around to face him, she wrapped her arms tightly around herself and said, "That's right."

"You don't look like a witch."

Her skin was dark, but not as dark as Slocum had previously guessed. Now that she was closer to him, he could

90

see the light brown hue that made her look vaguely Chinese, but not quite. Her eyes were slanted a bit and her face had the narrowness of a Chinese woman's. Her features, on the other hand, were far from the delicate lines of a China doll. On the contrary, the way she carried herself and glared at him made her look more like a cat. Long, coal black hair flowed straight down her back, and was tucked under the collar of her shirt so perfectly that Slocum hadn't even noticed it until she'd turned her back to him.

"What does a witch look like?" she asked.

Slocum blinked, pressed his shoulders against a wall, and slid down to have a seat on the floor. "I don't rightly know because there ain't no such thing as witches."

"Yes, there are," she said. "You just don't know any better."

Her voice had something of an accent to it, but Slocum couldn't place what kind it was. He'd heard plenty of Chinese during his time spent in California or in railroad camps, but that wasn't quite it. "Where are you from?" he asked.

"New York."

"Another surprise for the night," Slocum sighed. "At least that one was better than getting knocked on the head and dragged to jail."

She smiled and followed Slocum's lead by sitting on the floor against the wall across from him. "I was born in New York, but my parents aren't from there."

"Where are they from?"

As she thought about it, her face took on a darker quality that had nothing to do with the shadows filling the cramped confines of the box. Actually, it was the first time that Slocum had fully realized they were in the dark. He was close enough to see the exotic woman pretty well in the bit of light trickling in from outside, and other than her, there just wasn't much else to see.

"What about an easier question?" Slocum asked. "Like your name. Mine's John."

"Minh."

"Is that short for Minnie?"

She smiled and shook her head. "No. It's just Minh."

"And how'd you go about becoming a witch? Is there a special school for that like for doctors?"

"No. I taught myself all I needed to know."

"Well, you might want to consider finding somewhere else to practice your craft, because folks around here seem to be scared to death of you."

Minh raised her head and fixed her eyes upon Slocum. Her narrow features had been pretty a few moments ago. Now that her smile had disappeared, however, she looked hollow and cold. "That is how it should be."

Slocum had heard plenty of tough talk coming from plenty of folks. He knew it served a purpose, and figured Minh had one of her own. What he couldn't believe was just how good this skinny little woman was at putting a chill into a grown man. Slocum felt that chill work all the way through him before he shook it off the way a wet dog shakes off the rain.

"I'm not scared of you," he told her. "Perhaps that makes me different from these other folks."

After a few seconds, Minh said, "Yes, John. You are different." She leaned forward and stretched out both arms. Due to the cramped quarters, it wasn't long before she was on hands and knees and practically nose-to-nose with Slocum. "You really did kill a man."

"Yeah. Plenty of men."

"I can see the death upon you."

"What's that supposed to mean?" he asked.

From the moment she'd crawled away from the other side of the box, Minh never took her eyes away from Slocum's. She stared at him as if she could see straight through to his soul. Even though Slocum still didn't believe in such things, he had to admit there was something peculiar about this little woman.

"It means," she told him, "that I believe the two of us can get out of this place."

"What then? We run? Head to Mexico?" Slocum asked. "That might be just fine for a witch, but I'd rather not give the law more reasons to hunt me down."

"Westlake is my home. I will not leave. If I escape from here, they do not have the courage to hunt me down. And if they do, I'll just get out again."

"You sound like you've done this before."

"I have," Minh told him. "Four and a half times before."

Slocum chuckled, but didn't have much room to move with her so close to him. "What was the half?"

"The man who captured me let me go before I was thrown into a cage."

"Ah. I suppose that wouldn't count as a full escape, now would it? If you want to talk some more, you might want to sit back down."

"Why? Are you uncomfortable?"

"Not exactly," Slocum admitted. "Fact is, I'm getting a bit too comfortable. With you and me in such close quarters, it might be best if there was some distance between us. At least, more distance than this."

Slocum could feel heat from the little sigh that Minh let out as she curled half of her mouth into a smile. "You like having me so close. I can feel it."

There wasn't any black magic involved with that guess. Minh had slid her knee forward until her thigh brushed between Slocum's legs. From there, she couldn't have missed the fact that he was very happy about something or other.

"I do like having you so close," Slocum said. "But unless you intend to do something about it, I'd suggest you give me some breathing room. I'm only a man, you know."

"I do know. That's what I'm counting on. We can get out of here, but I need your help."

"I'm already wanted for killing someone, lady. You're

in here for bein' a witch. It might be best if we both just cooled our heels and stopped making waves."

"Nobody will look in on us for a while," she whispered.

"Are you certain of that?"

"Yes. I've been in here before. What's the matter? Are you sure you're not afraid of me?"

"Not afraid," Slocum replied. "I just don't want to get all riled up for no reason."

Minh worked the series of hooks that kept the front of her simple blouse closed and allowed it to fall open. "Is that a good enough reason for you?"

Slocum's only concern was that she was trying to get close to him so she could put him down and be alone in that box. Then he reminded himself that she could have attacked him plenty of times already and hadn't. Also, she was obviously thinking of plenty of other things besides fighting just then. That's when Slocum realized he had his guard up just a bit too high for his own good.

Minh's breasts were small, pert, and capped with little nipples that resembled chocolate drops. Her skin was the color of burnt sand and was smooth to the touch. In fact, as Slocum ran his hands under her shirt and over her body, he didn't want to take her clothes off. Her breasts fit nicely into his hands and when he massaged them, Minh let out a slow, throaty moan.

"That feels so good," she sighed.

Rubbing her breasts until the nipples became hard against his palms, Slocum said, "It sure does."

As he continued to feel her body, Minh slipped her legs around him and ground her hips against Slocum's growing erection. She then reached up to place her hands against the wall behind Slocum's head so she could move her breasts close to his mouth. Slocum didn't waste any time before he wrapped his arms around her waist and leaned forward to taste her skin. Minh's flesh had a distinctive flavor that was as exotic as she looked. Slocum ran his tongue between her breasts and then nibbled on one of her nipples.

As she felt his tongue and teeth on her skin, Minh pulled open Slocum's pants and lowered them enough to free his rigid pole. Slocum moved his hands down to feel between her legs. She wore a pair of buckskins that hugged her hips like a second skin. A rope was fastened around her waist as a makeshift belt, but Slocum was able to untie it and pull her pants down. Minh took it from there and kicked off her buckskins so the only clothing she wore was the blouse that hung off her shoulders.

Minh didn't waste any time before she straddled him. Slocum looked down to see the smooth, dark skin of her belly, and down a bit farther until he found the patch of hair between her legs. Minh wasn't bashful in the slightest. She reached down to stroke Slocum's cock before using that same hand to move the lips of her pussy apart enough to accommodate him. She was a slender little thing, but Minh enveloped Slocum nicely. Once he was inside her, she lowered herself on him until she'd taken in every last inch.

Keeping her hands on the wall behind Slocum's head, Minh began to rock back and forth. When Slocum held on to her hips to move her even faster, she moaned in a language that he'd never heard. Rather than try to figure out what she was saying, he just watched her petite face as she chanted and moaned.

Slocum sat up and scooted a little ways from the wall. Both of them were in the middle of the floor, facing each other. Minh's legs curled around him and he held on to her with both arms while pumping his hips in a slowly building rhythm.

Every part of Minh's body was tight and warm. The muscles in her back, legs, and stomach felt like bands of iron under her skin. Her pussy gripped his cock to make every movement something that he could feel all the way down to his toes. When he pumped into her a little faster, she thrust her hips back and forth to match his pace.

He could tell she was getting close to a climax, because Minh clung on to him even tighter. She dug her fingernails into Slocum's back and muttered her strange words into his ear. After one more powerful thrust, Minh gasped and fell silent. Her muscles twitched and her hips froze in their position.

Slocum waited for a few seconds and when he started to move, he felt Minh tremble even harder. He eased out of her a bit, waited, and then drove all the way in one more time. That caused Minh to lean back as far as she could and let out a loud string of words. While Slocum might not have known exactly what the words were, he knew they were in his favor.

Eventually, Minh opened her eyes and leaned back as far as she could. Propping herself up with both arms behind her, Minh moved her hips in a slow, gyrating motion. Watching Slocum intently, she pumped her hips quickly a few times as if she was curious to see what he would do.

Slocum leaned back, but couldn't go far before his shoulders bumped against the wall. The cramped quarters weren't easy to maneuver in, but all he needed to do was slide in and out of her and watch the way Minh's body moved as she rode his cock. From his angle, Slocum got a real good look at the lines of her trim body and the taut curves of her torso. Minh's blouse fell all the way open, giving him a perfect view of her pert little breasts. Beads of sweat rolled between them, running all the way down her stomach to either slide along her hips or collect in the dampness between her legs.

"Jesus," Slocum muttered as he felt his own climax swiftly approaching.

Picking up on that immediately, Minh smiled and moved her hips faster. She rested her head against the wall as her entire body took on an almost serpentine motion. Slocum just enjoyed the ride as she slid her wet pussy up and down along the length of his shaft.

She even seemed to know the exact moment that he reached his peak, because she suddenly sat up and took hold of his shoulders. Slocum opened his eyes to find her glaring intently at him. Her body continued to move, but her face remained perfectly still until she'd finally pushed him over the edge.

When Slocum exploded inside her, every muscle in his body tightened.

Minh made short little motions with her hips as if prolonging his orgasm as much as possible.

Just as Slocum thought he'd had enough, she tightened around him again to take him to another level.

To his surprise, he felt his cock grow harder inside her after only a few more seconds. He wrapped an arm around her waist and thrust into her with his newly discovered strength. This time, he was in charge and he acted out of nothing but raw instinct.

Slocum lay Minh on her back and climbed on top of her. She spread her legs open so wide that she propped her feet against the confining walls of the box around her. Her eyes widened as Slocum entered her again and immediately began pumping in and out. The urge was primal and constant, growing like wildfire with every thrust.

Minh let out a string of her peculiar words as her entire body shuddered with pleasure. Her muscles clenched and sweat poured from her skin as Slocum pounded into her again and again.

Reaching around to cup her backside, Slocum felt the tight curve of her buttocks perfectly fill his hand. He thrust into her while pulling her close, eased out, and then drove in again as deeply as he could. The moment he got all the way inside, he felt a second wave rush through him. It wasn't as powerful as the first, but it took damn near every bit of breath out of him. When it was done, his entire body could finally relax.

As Slocum sat up, he rubbed a hand over his face and pulled in a deep breath as if he'd just woken up from a fever dream.

Minh scooted toward the opposite wall and drew her legs up close to her body. She bent her knees, but kept them far enough apart to give Slocum a lingering view of her glistening little pussy. Smiling as if she knew every last thing going through his mind, Minh pulled her blouse so it barely covered her breasts.

"I don't know how that might help us get out of here," Slocum said, "but I sure ain't about to complain."

Minh smiled hungrily back at him. There was something in her eyes that was both sensual and disturbing at the same time. Slocum had heard of insects that ate their partners right after mating, and he guessed they might have a similar look in their eyes as well.

"That was necessary," she replied.

"Necessary for what?"

Slowly, Minh shifted her eyes toward the door that was locked up so tightly it could barely be distinguished from the wall. "Certain shamans and practitioners of black magic believe in using such ways to unlock parts of their spirit to be used in their craft."

"I've met a shaman or two in my time, but they sure as hell never did anything like that. It was usually more along the lines of smoking peyote or starving until the visions came."

"The rituals are different for different spells."

"Spells?"

She shrugged and said, "Call them whatever you like. Recipes, charms . . ."

"Curses?" Slocum asked. "I've been hearing that word tossed around quite a bit lately."

Minh smirked. "I've done my share of curses as well."

Just then, Slocum could hear movement from outside the box. The footsteps were close enough for him to hear since he had his head against the wall.

"When they come, I want you to stay where they cannot see you," she whispered.

Slocum looked around the small enclosed space. "Where the hell might that be?"

Minh pointed to the door itself. "Right there," she told him. "When they look in, they will only see me. That's all I want them to see."

Despite the fact that he still had a hard time acknowledging a witch with a straight face, Slocum scrambled around until he was sitting with his back against the door. He drew up his legs so if whoever was coming did look through the small window cut into the door, they probably wouldn't see him. "I doubt this'll fool anyone," Slocum grumbled, "but it's as good as I can do."

"That will be good enough," she said as she got to her feet and stood facing the door. "Now just keep quiet."

Slocum huddled under the opening, feeling like a complete idiot. The only thing that made it easier to bear was the fact that Minh stood up close to the door, which also put her less than an inch from his face. She was still naked from the waist down and her blouse hung loosely over her tight little frame.

The footsteps from outside drew closer, and then finally came to a stop less than half a yard away. "What's goin' on in there?" asked a man that Slocum recognized as the deputy who'd been partial to carrying a shotgun. "I heard noise."

"What noise?" Minh asked.

Although Slocum was looking at her from an odd angle, he still couldn't miss the change that had come over Minh's face. She wore a tired, sexy smile that aroused Slocum's instinct to grab her and pick up right where they'd left off.

Judging by the strain in the deputy's voice, he was feeling its effects as well.

"Uhhh . . . is there any trouble?" the deputy asked.

She shook her head, causing her straight black hair to dance around her face. "No. I just want to get out."

"I bet you do."

Sitting where he was, with his face so close to her bare thighs, Slocum had to struggle to keep from leaning forward and tasting her. He wanted nothing more than to just slide his hands up and down her skin. When he pulled in a breath, the air was filled with the scent of her.

"Just let me out for a few seconds," she whispered. "All I want is some fresh air."

"Wh . . . what about the fellow in there with you? Is he . . . did he . . . ?"

"He's asleep. Please," Minh said. "If you let me out, I'll repay you."

"Don't give me any of that," the deputy countered, even though there wasn't an ounce of strength behind his words. "I'm a . . . a married man."

Now Slocum had to keep himself from laughing. Not only did the deputy sound too weak to talk, but he also sounded as if he would have been hard-pressed to imagine his wife's face.

Minh smiled in a way that promised plenty of good things to come. "I can make you feel things your wife never could," she purred. "But if you don't want that, I can owe you a favor. It can be anything you like. Anything at all . . . at any time you want it. A favor from me can go a long way. You know that."

There was a shuffling outside. When the deputy spoke again, Slocum swore the other man was close enough to stick his face through the little square hole in the door.

"I can't just let you out."

"Of course you can," Minh replied. "Isn't that why you

came here? Aren't you supposed to check on how I am and if I need anything before you leave me here overnight?"

"I . . . suppose."

"Then let me have a breath of air," Minh said as she raised herself up onto her tiptoes so her face was within an inch of the deputy's and her hips were less than an inch from Slocum's nose. "Just for a second."

There was something about the combination of the smooth tone of Minh's voice and the exotic scent of her skin that made Slocum wonder if even *he* could have refused a request from her at that moment. He wasn't sure if it was witchcraft, but it was enough to make the deputy crack in a matter of seconds.

"Yeah," the lawman on the other side of the door said. "I can . . . I mean you can have a second, but then you'll go right back inside."

A key worked within the lock and the door swung loose before Slocum had a chance to move away from it. Without anything to support his back, Slocum rolled outside and pushed the door all the way open as he went. As the lawman tried to jump back, Slocum swept the deputy's legs out from under him.

There was a short tussle as the deputy tried to regain control and Slocum tried to get the lawman's gun away from him. The element of surprise tipped the scales in Slocum's favor, and he was able to end the struggle with a sharp jab to the deputy's face. Stunned and floundering, the deputy dropped his gun and immediately scrambled to retrieve it. Slocum got to the weapon first and pointed it right back at its owner.

The dull thump of iron meeting skull drifted through the air, followed by the impact of the deputy's limp body against the ground.

Minh stood in the doorway and whispered, "Bring him here. We can lock him inside."

Slocum dragged the unconscious deputy into the box. "There's going to be hell to pay for this. It might be better to wait for the others instead of making them come after us."

"The only one to get in trouble is him," she said as she nodded toward the lawman.

"You got a ritual for that, too?"

"No. I have escaped from these men several times and it is always the same. One makes a mistake and the others are too embarrassed to correct it. They are like animals. Stupid, predictable animals."

Slocum grinned, picked up Minh's pants, and handed them to her. "Lady, that's the most sense you've made all night."

10

They left the deputy in the box with the door slightly ajar. The lawman would have a headache when he woke up, but not much else. He sure wouldn't have his shotgun. Minh wanted to go back to her home and clean up. Considering it was well past midnight and there wasn't even enough of a moon in the sky to let him see three inches past his nose, Slocum went along with her. After all, he'd never gotten the chance to see where a witch lived.

As it turned out, witches lived like most other folks. She had a little cabin on the side of a hill just outside of town. It wasn't completely hidden from sight, but was built along a stretch of land that most locals tended to avoid. When Slocum saw the peculiar designs painted on the posts leading up to the cabin and the collections of bones strung from the trees, he got a better idea of why most folks stayed away.

Inside, the cabin was less threatening. There was a small bed covered by several blankets and a pillow encased in silk. A table big enough for maybe two people was set up next to a little stove and a few cabinets where some food was stored. In another corner was a rolltop desk that could have been just as suited for a hotel lobby or accountant's office.

The other half of the cabin was where things got a little

more interesting. What looked like a second kitchen at first was actually a spot where supplies more exotic than flour and sugar were stored. The jars Slocum spotted there weren't filled with preserves, and he sure as hell wouldn't eat anything from any of them. At least, not voluntarily anyway. When he headed over there for a closer look, Slocum was stopped by a single sharp word.

"Don't," Minh snapped.

Slocum stopped in mid-stride and turned around. "Why not? You afraid I might ruin one of your spells?"

"I just don't want you poking through my things."

"All right," Slocum said with a shrug. "I can accept that. Does the law know where this place is? They might want to sift through some of these things sooner or later."

"Everyone knows where I live. They leave me alone and that's the way I like it."

"You don't seem too worried. Then again, I suppose if you've escaped so many times before, you've probably got this all worked out to a nice little system."

Minh walked over to the section of the cabin taken up by her bed and a small dresser. "You sound like you don't believe what I told you."

"I've had plenty of experience with the law, and they never take too kindly to folks who knock out a deputy and walk out of jail."

"You knocked the deputy out," Minh pointed out as she selected a long dress that looked to be made from tanned deerskin.

Slocum crossed his arms and asked, "What did you expect me to do?"

"Exactly what you did. Just don't blame me for it." Keeping her eyes on him, Minh peeled off her clothes and turned around to arrange them neatly upon her bed. The lines of her trim body were still impressive from a distance. When she bent slightly at the waist, Slocum took in the sight of her tight little backside.

"Come on now," he said. "Be honest with me. You may have talked your way out of a few scrapes, but you couldn't have escaped from jail more than once. Nobody would stand for it."

As if sensing Slocum's eyes on her, Minh kept her back to him and wriggled into the dress a little slower than seemed necessary. "Despite what folks think or what they say . . . even what they believe . . . there is no judge that will accuse me of being a witch. There are some old laws still on the books, but the only people who enforce them are fools and vigilantes. So far," she said as she turned around and tugged at the sides of her dress to straighten them out, "both of those also tend to be too frightened of me to make good on their threats."

Slocum could have stood there looking at Minh for hours. She wasn't exactly the first woman he'd ever seen, but he just couldn't pull his eyes away from her. It took some effort on his part, but Slocum managed to do so anyhow. Judging by the smirk that appeared on Minh's face, she knew exactly how difficult that had been for him.

"Yeah," Slocum grunted, "but the law doesn't shy away from men like me who get one over on them. When that deputy wakes up, he'll be calling for blood."

"Tell them I made you do it," Minh offered. "They will believe you."

"They might, but I don't know how much I like the idea of hiding behind any woman's skirts."

"You could ride away then. You should have a good head start before—"

"No," Slocum said quickly. "I won't run either."

Minh shrugged, and walked over to the corner where all the interesting jars were stored. "Then you don't leave yourself with many options."

"I was given one option before I was tossed into that box. The deputy told me to kill you and he'd set me free."

Holding one of the jars in her hand, Minh nodded slowly

and then dipped her hand into what looked like a gritty mixture of sand and some sort of bleached white rocks. "There are some who believe killing a witch will bring misfortune that will follow you to your grave."

"Killing anyone tends to follow you like that. For some of us, one more ghost won't make much difference."

"Are you threatening me?" Minh asked.

There was no fear in her voice. There also wasn't any attempt to put fear into him. It was just a simple question of life and death.

After a bit of consideration, Slocum patted his hip and said, "I don't even have my gun. I'm not in a spot to threaten anyone."

"I know better than that. There are more ways to kill than with a gun." As she said those words, Minh's fingers drifted through the grit in the jar.

Slocum couldn't help but wonder what sort of uses she had in mind for that concoction. "You've got some tricks up your sleeve, that's for certain," he said. "I still don't believe in witches, and curses only work because folks let them work. Hell, I've seen Indians dance over someone until they're healed from sickness or bullet wounds. You ask me, that's just because the sick person put so much faith in all that dancing. The same thing could be said for folks who go to church and claim to have a cleaner soul."

"Speak ill of the church and you'll be stricken by a different sort of curse," Minh warned.

"I don't bear any grudges against the church," he said, "just like I don't bear any ill will toward them shamans. Say whatever you want about either one, but they mostly mean well and that's all that matters. What I'm trying to say is that all I've seen so far don't amount to black magic or any sort of witchcraft. All the scribbling on barn doors and talk of curses is just that. Scribbles and talk."

"I set us both free using my useless talk."

"No," Slocum said. "You used the charms that were given to all women."

Minh walked slowly toward him, but didn't remove her hand from the jar until it was absolutely necessary. "Have you seen anyone bend a man's mind the way I have?"

"No. Then again, there's a gal in Saint Louis who can do things with her tongue that I ain't never seen repeated. That don't make her a witch."

Minh flinched, looked down, and then laughed. The simple reaction made her look like a completely different woman.

"Whatever you're doing," Slocum continued, "it's got everyone in this town fooled. From what I've seen, you've got some real talents and you sure know how to put them to use. It may be a con or it may be the real thing. I don't profess to know a real witch when I see one. What I do know is that men around here want to see you dead and they're gonna get their way sooner or later."

Shaking her head, Minh replied, "They talk and talk, but they are too frightened to even approach my home."

"Then they'll hire someone who isn't so frightened. Hell, they might just get close enough to toss a few torches your way and burn your home to the ground."

"They tried when I first arrived. Now some of the people who say the worst things about me are the ones who pay me the most for my wares." Turning on the balls of her bare feet, Minh walked over to one row of jars and pointed them out one by one. "I sell love potions, wards against rats, and charms to bring money to new businesses. I find lost things and make others disappear forever."

When she turned around again, Minh found herself less than a foot away from Slocum. She pulled in a quick breath and started to back away, but was stopped when Slocum snapped a hand out to close around her arm.

Keeping her in place, Slocum said, "You also take money

to curse ranchers. You use your reputation to walk out of jail. That's already crossing two sorts of men who don't like to be crossed. Sooner or later, one of them will get to you."

"I have friends here," she told him.

"When push comes to shove, will they stand up for a witch?"

Minh was stung by those words. She furrowed her brow and pulled her arm from Slocum's grip with a surprising amount of strength. "I don't need anyone to stand up for me."

"You can't rely on folks to stand back either. A lawman asked me to kill you."

"Are you going to try to kill me then?" she asked with a fiery glint in her eye.

Slocum shook his head. "No, but the next man who's asked may not think the same way I do. There are plenty of other men who kill for money, and the more you piss off rich men like Landry or even Hal Singer, the more money will be offered for someone to do that job. Even if nobody around here will step up to take that cash, someone will. You can bet all the potions you got on that."

"Someone has already tried," Minh said in a voice that was part whisper and part hiss. "When I first arrived to sell my wares, someone thought they would stop me by killing me. They were never seen again."

"Let me guess," Slocum said. "You brought some fella with you to help get you settled in. Maybe he was a friend or just someone you hired, but he made a public spectacle of calling you out and then you made an even bigger spectacle in getting rid of him. He leaves town and you make up a good story about why he left. Am I close?"

Minh leaned forward and spoke in a steady stream of words that seemed to come from a rock. She didn't blink and she didn't flinch as she told him, "I displayed his head on a pike in front of my home until the animals gnawed it away."

Slocum leaned forward a bit as well. "Could'a been a body dug up from anywhere that you cut apart and used to make a display. The only one that knows any different is the one who's missing a head, and he ain't exactly in a condition to dispute your claims."

Her face remained an unmoving mask. "You do not know enough to call me a liar."

"Liar may be a bit strong," Slocum admitted. "You may or may not be a witch, but I know you're stretching things with this story you just told me."

"How do you know that?"

"Because killing a man takes sand, and not the kind that you can collect in any jar," he told her while extending an arm toward Minh's exotic collection. "And do you have any idea how hard it is to cut off a man's head? Do you have any idea how long it takes to saw through all that meat and all that thick bone? Can you imagine how much blood sprays everywhere?"

Slocum paused so he could study her. For the first time, he detected some hesitation on Minh's part. She wanted to look away from him, but wouldn't allow herself to do so. Even so, the spark in her eyes was just a little dimmer than it had been a few moments ago.

"I've killed plenty of men," Slocum continued. "I've killed them in plenty of different ways. Sometimes, it seems like killing is easy, but I would never think to saw off someone's head. And, after all of that, mounting the head on a damn pike? That couldn't have been easy even way back when folks really did that sort of thing."

"Ask anyone who lived here at that time," Minh said in a challenging tone. "They'll tell you it was there."

Slocum nodded, and then looked out one of the windows as if he could see the mounted skull in question. "Getting your hands on a body . . . that's a gruesome task, but you could manage it. Cutting the poor dead man's head off? That's a whole different thing than doing it when the blood's still warm." Looking around again, Slocum asked, "Where is it now? If you went through all that trouble, surely you'd keep the skull or bones around for decorations? Maybe hang 'em over your door or use 'em for some spell or such? Or did you get sick and tired of looking at it? Would a witch develop a weak stomach?"

"I have a heart," Minh told him. "I do not want to be surrounded with death."

"That's right," Slocum said. "Like I already told Hal Singer, I can spot a killer's eyes. That's a little trick that's kept me alive for a hell of a long time. Lady, I'll believe you're a witch before I believe you're some cold-blooded killer."

"Why do you insist on arguing with what you see in front of you?" Minh asked as she held out her hands to motion toward the jars as well as the strange items hanging from her walls and ceiling.

"I'm just pointing out what I do see. Come to think of it, I'm glad you've gone through so much effort to get yourself established so nicely."

Minh cocked her head to one side and scowled at him. "Why are you glad?"

"Because you've done a hell of a good job. Whether you're a genuine witch or just a slick talker, you've got this whole town eating from the palm of your hand. If you truly got the law whipped into shape like you say you do, we could both stand to make a killing of a different sort."

"Have you not seen enough to convince you of that at least?"

"Almost," Slocum replied. "But I wouldn't mind seeing just a bit more."

11

The next morning arrived like any other. The sun rose, the air warmed up, folks started going about their business. As far as Westlake was concerned, this wasn't much different than all the days that had come before it.

Slocum walked down one street after another, taking in the sights and sounds as if he was a complete stranger to the place. He might not have spent more than a month at the Singer ranch, but he'd been into Westlake enough times to be recognized by a few people. For him, though, the town seemed a lot different.

Not only had he learned about a witch that had supposedly been living there the entire time, but he'd been given a very unique look at the town's law. While Slocum didn't exactly hold lawmen in the highest esteem anyway, he'd at least figured Sheriff Bilson was more lazy than stupid. Judging by the calm in the air after such an eventful night, Slocum figured he could add superstitious to that list as well.

Before too long, Slocum picked up on the scent of bacon being fried and of eggs being cooked. He wandered into a hotel on the corner that was the source of those scents. Tipping his hat to the old woman behind the front desk, Slocum walked back to where the food was being served and picked out a seat. Within moments, the sister of the old woman from the front desk walked over to set a cup down in front of him.

"Are you a guest here?" she asked.

"No, ma'am," Slocum told her. "I just haven't had any breakfast yet. Can you spare some bacon and eggs?"

She smiled. "Of course. I'll bring it right over to you."

Slocum was served some coffee first, which he finished as his plate was brought out to him. When the old woman was refilling his cup, he asked, "Was there any commotion last night?"

"Commotion? Here?"

"Not at this hotel, but in town. I heard there was some sort of fight down at the Bull's Horn."

"Oh, there's a fight at one of those saloons every night," she said with a dismissive wave. "Boys will be boys. I did hear that the sheriff had his hands full, though."

Pretending as if he didn't already know that, Slocum raised his eyebrows and said, "Is that so?"

"It sure is." The old woman lowered her voice and eagerly looked around to make sure none of the other guests were listening. "I heard from the sheriff himself that some of the troublemaking cowboys who work for Mr. Landry and Mr. Singer were rounded up and spent the night in jail."

Not only did Slocum already know where the town law ate their breakfast, but he'd avoided the hotel for the same reason. That played in his favor for the moment, since the old woman hadn't seen his face enough to know that he was one of those troublemaking cowboys. "Sounds terrible," he said.

"More terrible for them," she continued. "They had to stew in that jailhouse with . . ." Suddenly, the old woman stopped and looked down at Slocum once more. The longer she stared at him, the more uncomfortable she became.

"Yes?" Slocum asked. "They were with someone else?"

"Just some other filthy drunks that were rounded up,"

she quickly said. "That jailhouse probably stinks to high heaven by now."

Slocum wanted to press her on what she'd really meant to say. He wanted to see if the old woman would actually mention that a witch had been locked in the jail with those men and that was why she figured the poor drunks had been put through the wringer. More than anything, Slocum wanted to bring up those things just to see how much the woman would squirm. Instead, he bit his tongue. He'd already gotten the answers he needed, along with a hint as to how he'd lived so close to Westlake for as long as he had without hearing any mention of a witch.

"Do you need anything else?" the woman asked.

"No. I got what I need."

Assuming he meant his breakfast, the old woman nodded and walked away.

Slocum ate his meal at his own pace, spending a good amount of time looking out the hotel's front window. While he wasn't an expert in jailbreaks, he figured there would be a bit more commotion after one had happened. As far as he could tell, things were moving along as they always did. There were no lawmen scouring the streets for a trace of the missing prisoners. There were no notices tacked to any walls. There wasn't even any loose talk about escaped criminals roaming free.

When Minh told him how the law tiptoed around her, Slocum had guessed she was just making herself look good. Now he wasn't so sure.

After finishing his last bite of bacon, Slocum paid for his meal and walked outside. He worked his way down one street and up another, nodding to the familiar faces and taking note of all the others. It wasn't until he got within a block of the sheriff's office that he so much as noticed a single man wearing a badge. There sure wasn't any guesswork in figuring out when one of those men noticed him.

"Holy shit! That's him!" the young man wearing the badge exclaimed as he pointed wildly down the street.

Slocum walked slowly toward the deputy. Even though he didn't have a gun at his side, he kept his arms out where they could be easily seen. He even reached up to tip his hat to the younger man.

"Don't move!" the deputy shouted.

Slocum could hear the panic in the young lawman's voice even from twenty yards away. "Take it easy," Slocum said. "If I wanted to cause any trouble, I wouldn't have walked straight toward—"

"Shut yer damn mouth and stay still!"

Letting out a measured breath, Slocum raised his arms and stood perfectly still.

Within seconds, more deputies converged on the first one and then fanned out to walk directly toward Slocum. On either side of the street, locals stopped what they were doing and watched the scene while excitedly chattering to one another.

"You got any guns?" the first deputy asked.

"Not on me," Slocum replied. "But I'd like to have mine back."

"I just bet you would."

Slocum was roughly searched and then pushed down the street toward the sheriff's office. By the time they climbed the two steps leading from the street to the sheriff's door, the locals were already getting back to what they'd been doing before the show.

It took every bit of restraint Slocum had to keep from shaking loose of the deputies and putting them in their place. Although that would have made him feel a little better after everything that had happened, he reminded himself of why he was there in the first place. When he thought of what was coming, the rest was easier to take.

Slocum hadn't been into the sheriff's office until just now, but it wasn't any different than what he'd expected.

There were a few cluttered desks that showed a bit too much use by men who should have spent more of their days outside. There were some gun cabinets packed with double the firepower a lawman in a town like Westlake would need, and, of course, there was the sheriff himself.

Bilson sat behind his desk, trying to look as if he'd been caught in the middle of something important. When he glanced up at Slocum, the asshole was even wearing reading glasses. "There you are, Slocum," he said. "I thought you'd left town for good."

"Perhaps I just wandered off," Slocum said. "After all, I did get a knock on the head from some bastard who was too yellow to look me in the eye."

Gritting his teeth, Bilson stood up and rested his hand on the smoke wagon holstered at his side. "You killed a man. I don't treat killers with a delicate touch."

"How about telling a man why he's being arrested? Or introducing yourself," Slocum added. "That might have caused things to go a lot smoother."

Suddenly, Bilson waved his free hand as if he was trying to shoo a foul odor out the window. "What's done is done. I see you had the good sense to come back, so maybe I was wrong in thinking you might not have come to see me if I cordially requested your presence."

Slocum wasn't sure if the sheriff was wrong about that, but it wouldn't have helped him any to point that out.

"Take a load off," Sheriff Bilson said. "Since you came in to face me like a man, I won't toss you directly back into the jailhouse until you've said your piece. I gather you came back to say something or other."

"That's right." As Slocum sat down, he shifted in the chair as though he expected to get bitten by it. "I figured it might be easier to come have a word with you, seeing as how there's a man dead and all."

"Tell me what happened with that."

Slocum described the events in short order, only touching

on the major points. He finished with, "They all had guns aimed at me. One of them was gonna shoot, so I shot him first."

"Sounds about right. He was a pudgy fellow, wasn't he? A bit shorter than you."

"That's the one."

Bilson nodded. "That'd be Paul. He never did know when to ease back on the throttle. Whenever he had a bunch of them others backing him up, he got a real big mouth on him. Got real violent a couple of times, too."

"So where does that leave us?" Slocum asked. "One of your deputies told me I was to be hung."

"As far as that matter's concerned, it's a clear case of a man defending himself. No law against that. As for my deputy, he was speaking out of turn."

Slocum glanced around nervously as if he was still waiting for something bad to happen. Even though nothing did, the knot in his gut remained. "So that's it?"

Bilson nodded. "Unless you wanted to take it up with Landry. But I mediated a truce between those two ranchers and he's willing to drop the matter altogether."

"So a deal's already been struck?"

"It sure has."

Slocum's eyes widened as a few of the pieces fell together. "And the stolen property?"

Spreading out his hands as though he was smoothing out a rumpled blanket, the sheriff replied, "It's all been straightened out. Mr. Singer told me that you brought in some impressive evidence that Landry had those animals stolen. I hear you even got Landry to admit as much himself."

"Yeah. That happened right around when the guns came out."

Nodding slowly, Bilson continued in a level tone that was normally reserved for politicians. "That news took the wind out of Landry's sails. Word got back that the animals were returned . . . from both sides of the fence I might add . . . and both parties agreed to call it a draw."

"A draw, huh?" Slocum asked. "A few cows and horses get shuffled around, a man dies, and some more wind up in jail, but so long as the two men in the fancy suits say so, it's a friendly draw."

"Would you rather prolong the fight?"

"I would have rather avoided getting my skull split."

"I feel bad about that," Bilson said, even though the subtle grin on his face told a much different story. "But I was approaching a killer and there were innocents about. Surely, you understand."

"Yeah," Slocum grunted. "I guess I do."

As the conversation had gone on, more of the deputies had drifted back into the office to stand and watch. Although their guns were mostly holstered, there was still at least one shotgun in the open.

"If things are all square, when do I get my gun back?" Slocum asked.

The sheriff reached for a drawer in his desk and pulled it open. "How about right now?" he said as he took out the entire rig and set it on his desk.

Slocum picked up his gun belt and quickly examined it. The Colt Navy was right where it should be, and even the extra bullets looped into the belt were all accounted for.

"And don't forget these," Bilson said as he reached back into the drawer to remove the bullets that had been taken from the Colt's cylinder. "Wouldn't be the same without 'em."

Gathering up the bullets, Slocum tested the waters by simply moving the bullets close to the Colt. Sure enough, the deputies all tensed like bowstrings being drawn tight. Slocum didn't have any intention of pushing his luck too far, but he kept the bullets near the gun just to see how long the lawmen would all hold their breath.

Finally, Slocum dropped the bullets into his shirt pocket and then draped the gun belt over his shoulder. "By the way, I seem to recall there was some other offer made as I was being shown into that box."

Bilson didn't even flinch. "That's right. According to Nate, that job still needs to be done."

Slocum looked around until he spotted the deputy that had been drooling over Minh just long enough to unlock the door to let her out. "How's your head?" he asked.

The deputy did a good job of holding his chin up, but the bandages could still be seen poking out from under his hat. "No better than yours."

"The offer that was made," the sheriff said, "is the only reason I don't peel yer hide off your bones for laying a finger on one of my men. Did you get the job done?"

"I had to come back here to make certain the offer was genuine," Slocum explained. "Wouldn't want to be brought in for a second killing."

"It's genuine. Is it done or isn't it?"

"Not yet."

"So you just decided to kick dirt in my face by striking one of my men so you could just ride away as you pleased?" Bilson asked. "Maybe coming back here wasn't such a good idea for you after all." As he said that, Bilson motioned toward his deputies, and Nate was the one to step forward. "Take this man outta my sight."

Nate stepped up to Slocum and dropped a hand on his shoulder. When Slocum didn't move right away, Nate tightened his grip and started to pull Slocum up from the chair. At least, Nate *tried* to pull Slocum from his chair.

With a quick snap of his right hand, Slocum knocked away Nate's arm. Not only was the blow strong enough to break the deputy's grip, but it put one hell of a surprised look onto Nate's face. The moment Nate moved to reassert himself, Slocum looked back at him and said, "Putting that hand on me again is a real good way to lose it."

"And walking into my office to spit in my face is a real good way to get your neck stretched," Sheriff Bilson said.

"What'd this woman ever do to you anyway?" Slocum asked.

Nate lingered behind Slocum's chair like a vulture waiting for a fresh kill to stop twitching. He backed up quickly enough when Bilson nodded in his direction.

"She's a witch," Bilson said. "Does it matter what else she's done?"

Being careful to keep his face steady and not grin when he spoke, Slocum asked, "And you really believe the witch part?"

"Plenty of folks in my town believe. She's stirred up more than enough trouble around here. She's even been known to accept money for what are either blasphemous charms or useless trinkets that are made to bilk good people out of their money. I don't give a shit if it's witchcraft or not. She's making trouble and profiting from it."

"So run her out of town," Slocum offered. "Why put a bounty on her head?"

"There's no official bounty on that woman's head."

This time, no amount of effort could keep Slocum from grinning. It always struck him as funny when a lawman would twist words around or fiddle with the letter of the law until it suited his purpose. That was only one reason why he instinctively distrusted any man wearing a badge, but it was a hell of a good one as far as Slocum was concerned.

"All right then," Slocum said. "Why let one of your deputies discreetly make me an offer to kill that woman?"

While Slocum didn't see much difference between that and a bounty, the sheriff was appeased by the new arrangement of words.

"That bitch tried to kill some of my men," Bilson said.

"Is that why she was in jail?"

"More or less." Bilson shifted in his chair, which looked a lot like a worm squirming at the end of a hook. "She poisoned one of my men after she made a shop owner so damn sick that he nearly died himself. The doctor couldn't figure out what poisoned either of them, but it sure as hell cleared up once the ransom was paid."

"Ransom, huh?"

"She called it a fee to pay for a potion or whatnot to clear up the sickness. I call it blood money that needed to be paid in order to keep someone from ending up dead. Ain't that a ransom to you?"

"Yeah," Slocum admitted. "I suppose it is. You don't seem too upset that she's no longer in your jailhouse."

"The truth of the matter is that I don't got the proof needed to put her up in front of a judge. Nothing she's ever done leaves a set of tracks like a normal crime. There ain't no gunshots, bloody knives, or anything else left behind, but some concoctions that nobody knows what to make of. There ain't no witnesses because they're all scared shitless of her. Hell, even upstanding businessmen around here would paint heathen markings on their walls to protect against that woman before they'd take any legal stand against her. I've tried scaring her, but she just plain don't get scared. Short of executing her outright myself, there's not a lot else I can do."

"You're the law around here," Slocum said. "You're supposed to think of something to do."

"I have. If someone doesn't take me up on my offer, I'll think of something a little more drastic." Leaning forward, Bilson added, "Don't presume to tell me my business. The only reason I've talked to you so long about this is because I got a hunch you know how to get close to that skinny, slant-eyed pain in my ass. She's slipped out of my jail before somehow, and that don't make me look good. Me and my men are the only ones that know about this last break-out, so deliver her to me in two days or I'll have to count you as a fugitive from justice. And, unlike our witch, you've got plenty of legitimate charges hanging over your head."

"And if I deliver her?" Slocum asked. "What happens with those charges then?"

"They go away," Bilson replied as he snapped his fingers. "Just like that. You get some money in your pocket and we all go home happy. Once folks in this town realize they don't have to hold their breaths any longer on account of some goddamn ghost story, they won't ask questions about how she disappeared."

Slocum stood up and turned so he could get a look at all the other men in that office. "So," he said as he slowly shifted his eyes from one face to another, "you've just let her get away with breaking out of your jail because she's a witch? I wonder how the hell she got out all those times?"

If the men in that room had been better at keeping lies under their hats, they would have been professional card sharps instead of deputies in a little town like Westlake. As it was, Slocum could see at least two men who didn't like where that last question was headed, and another two who definitely wanted Slocum to keep his mouth shut. Being so familiar with Minh's tactics for getting men to help her, Slocum had a real good guess as to how she'd convinced the deputies to let her go the previous times.

"She escaped because she's a witch," Bilson said. "As far as anyone's concerned, that's the only explanation that's needed. She may have been a nuisance for a while, but she's moved all the way up the ladder to an embarrassment and threat to me and this town. She's gonna fall. I'd rather keep my hands clean of it, but if I have to, I'll hunt her down and burn her at the stake."

"That might get you some admirers from the superstitious folks in town," Slocum pointed out.

"It also might make me look like a goddamn idiot to anyone who might catch wind of what happened here. I got my sights set on bigger and better jurisdictions, and it don't do me a lick of good to be known as the man who killed some poor little slip of a woman on account of some stories."

And that was the last piece Slocum had been fishing for. Now that he'd learned everything he'd wanted to know, he buckled his gun belt around his waist and started walking toward the door. It was slow going, since his path was blocked by nearly every deputy in the office.

"So what's it gonna be?" Bilson asked.

Meeting the closest deputy's eyes, Slocum replied, "I know where to find your witch and I can make sure she's not a problem to you anymore. But it's gonna cost you more than you dropping a shooting charge that should be dropped anyhow."

"Five hundred dollars," the sheriff said. "That's what you get for her scalp."

"Make it a thousand."

"Done. Now get out of my sight and get to work."

As Slocum left that office, he cursed himself for a fool. He probably could have gotten at least another five hundred out of that slimy coward.

12

Not only did Slocum get his gun back, but he got his horse back as well. Upon leaving the sheriff's office, Slocum spotted his horse tied to a post across the street. It might have been there before, but he'd had bigger things on his mind when he was walking up the street a little earlier. Now his mind was a bit more at ease and he spotted the horse right away. Bilson hadn't said anything about allowing Slocum to take the horse back, but Slocum helped himself anyway. Apparently, if he needed to pass blame for the missing animal onto anyone else, Slocum could just mention the witch of Westlake.

He rode out of town and made sure nobody was trying to follow him. After letting his horse stretch its legs for a while at a full gallop, he steered for open terrain and headed back to the Singer Moon Ranch. He was spotted before too long by a pair of cowboys mending a length of broken fence.

"Slocum! We thought you'd be locked up for another couple of days!" hollered a ranch hand named Earl.

Now that he'd officially returned to friendlier ground, Slocum felt like he could finally stop looking over his shoulder. Jabbing a finger toward the man who stood next to Earl, Slocum said, "No thanks to that one right there. I think he

123

would've let me stew in that box for another year or two if it meant he was home in time for supper."

Mack shook his head and grumbled, "To hell with you, John. If standing up for you means gettin' tossed in a jailhouse and knocked around by drunks, you can ride on yer own for a while."

Slocum looked down at Mack and tipped his hat. "You stood your ground back there. I appreciate it."

"Don't think too highly of yerself. I'll take any reason I can to bloody the noses of some of them Landry boys."

"I wish I could'a been there," Earl chimed in. "Sounds like a real hoot."

Suddenly, Mack squinted and looked at Slocum as if he was inspecting him for ticks. "Wait a second. How the hell did you get out so quick?"

"Didn't you hear? I cracked a deputy upside the head and ran for the hills."

Both of the ranch hands laughed as they climbed onto their horses and steered toward the middle of the property. "I liked it better when you did your work and kept to yourself," Mack said. "Remember them days, Earl?"

"Yeah, but this is a lot more fun. I don't think Hal's stopped pacing for a full day."

"Has he been trying to plan the party he means to throw me once I got out from behind bars?" Slocum asked.

"Not hardly," Mack said. "Seems more like he's trying to figure out how he can get back into everyone's good graces so business can get back to normal."

"I'm only gone for half a day and he lets this place slide to hell?" Slocum asked.

"I don't know the details. All I know is what I heard when I went into the house to collect a few things. He's stompin' around his office, wearing a trench into the floorboards and shouting to God and everyone about losing time and money on account of this mess. By the mess, I expect

he meant you and me landing in the jailhouse when we
should'a been workin'."

Slocum dismissed that with a shrug. "Eh, it's hard to tell
anymore. There's plenty of messes around here lately."

After glancing over to study Slocum for a moment or
two, Mack said, "You don't look too unhappy about it."

"Hell," Earl added, "he looks downright chipper for a
man fresh out of the box."

Smirking in the face of those accusations, Slocum
replied, "Messes aren't my favorite thing, but there's always profit for the man who'll clean them up."

Earl chuckled. "You need anyone to help with that, look
no further. For a cut of the profit, we could—"

"Speak for yerself," Mack interrupted. "I got all the
work I need right here. Besides, drivin' cattle and mending
fences ain't as much of a headache as cleanin' up anything
that involves rich men and the law."

Even though Earl didn't seem to understand exactly what
his partner was saying, he shrugged and lost his enthusiasm
anyway. "I guess so. Mr. Singer probably wouldn't let me
take on any extra work till the rest of them fences are patched
up."

Slocum and Mack shot a quick glance at each other that
spoke volumes. Mack would steer Earl away from whatever was really going on, and Slocum wouldn't press the
matter any further. Earl was content to chatter about plenty
of other nonsense for the duration of the ride back to the
Singer family home. Once there, Slocum dismounted and
waved to the other two.

"I'll find you after supper, John," Mack said. "I want to
hear about what sins you committed to get out of that damn
box."

"I'll even make up a few extra ones to keep the story interesting."

Mack snapped his reins and rode to catch up with Earl.

Normally, unless they'd been specifically invited, ranch hands were expected to knock on the front door before entering Hal's home. After the night he'd had, Slocum didn't feel like bowing to every little rule. He didn't even feel like showing his employer an extra bit of courtesy as he pulled open the front door and stormed inside.

Kelly Singer was sitting in the room just off the entrance, and she jumped to her feet when she saw who'd arrived. "John! I heard you weren't coming back for a while."

"Is that all you heard?"

"Yes. Where were you?" Kelly asked as she played with the front of Slocum's shirt. "Didn't you miss me?"

"Sure. No matter what the hell else might have happened, the only thing I could think of was how much I missed you."

The dry tone in Slocum's voice was completely lost on her. Kelly smiled and even blushed a little, as though she'd just heard the very words she'd been praying would come from Slocum's mouth. She even looked more than a little surprised when Slocum pulled away from her.

"Where are you—" she started to ask, but stopped once she saw her uncle standing outside his office door.

"Slocum! I didn't send for you," Hal blustered.

"Well, I'm here anyway. No thanks to you, I might add."

The rancher's cheeks turned even redder than his niece's, but for a much different reason. Hal was so mad, he resembled a blister that was about to burst. "Get in here and stop fooling about with my niece!"

Just to get under Hal's skin, Slocum took a few steps toward the hall and then turned to shoot a quick smile in Kelly's direction. The smile worked. Seeing the excited little grin on her face made Hal that much madder. When Slocum walked past him to enter the office, the rancher followed and slammed the door hard enough to rattle the hinges. "Do you know what I had to do to make up for what you did?"

"From where I was sitting in that jailhouse," Slocum replied, "you weren't doing much of anything."

"You had to sit somewhere while I spoke to the sheriff about them animals you stole. Even though we returned 'em, there was still hell to pay."

"Oh, that."

"Yes. *That!*" Hal snarled as he pounded a fist against his desk. That same hand was trembling as he fished a cheroot out of the box and struck a lucifer to light it. "No sooner did I get that squared away than I hear you and Mack were rounded up for fighting!"

Slocum made himself comfortable in one of the chairs in front of Hal's desk. "Mack was fighting. I killed a man."

Hal clamped down on his cheroot almost hard enough to bite clean through it. "You think this is funny?"

"A little. Knowing that a whole town, the law, and even men like you and Landry are frightened of a witch is pretty funny. Once I got a look at the witch up close, it was even funnier. You know she's almost as skinny as those smokes you're always chewing on?"

"You saw the witch?" Hal asked casually.

Slocum nodded. "We got tossed into the box together. In case you don't know, the box is a woodshed that's so small a man can hardly breathe in it. I was meant to spend a good amount of time in there because my concerned employer didn't bother to pull any strings to get me out."

Suddenly, Hal didn't seem so concerned with displaying his temper. He cooled off quicker than a hot iron dunked into a bucket of water as he asked, "What did you expect me to do about it?"

"Maybe put a good word in for me while you and Landry were talking with the sheriff."

"We were discussing that and other matters."

"Like how much you needed to pay to keep the scuffle between your two ranches out of any legal trouble?"

Rather than dispute the claim, Hal replied, "Business is business."

Slocum nodded. "Yeah, I've heard that plenty of times

before. Where does that witch fit in? Is she part of business or just some way to get under Landry's skin?"

"Landry's a superstitious idiot. He believes in that nonsense, so I hired her to do a job. The more flustered he is, the better it works out for me."

"Did you know that witch is a burr under the sheriff's saddle as well?" Slocum asked. When he caught a glimpse of the smirk that flickered across Hal's face, he said, "I see that you do. Did he tell you I was tossed into that box with her?"

"I . . . may have heard something to that effect."

Slocum narrowed his eyes to study the rancher the way he'd studied the deputies in Bilson's office. And, like those younger lawmen, Hal couldn't sit still for long before he started to squirm.

"You knew about the offer to take care of her, didn't you?" Slocum asked.

"I . . . might have—"

"Spare me the bullshit," Slocum snapped.

Although it was plain to see that Hal wasn't accustomed to being spoken to that way, he didn't explode at Slocum the way he might blow up at any of his other employees if they'd taken that tone with him. On the contrary, Hal nodded slowly and seemed to relax a bit. "Fine. I knew about it."

"Did you arrange it?"

Slocum made the guess on a whim, but it paid off almost immediately.

"Perhaps I suggested you could straighten things out with her," Hal replied with a nod. "But that was only because I knew one of those deputies would give you a chance to become a rich man."

"The deputy asked me to kill her."

"And did you?"

"I thought you were working with that woman," Slocum pointed out. "It sounds like she did everything you paid her for."

"She's a damn witch!" Hal said emphatically. "I don't

give a damn how crazy it sounds, but it's true. I hired her to spook Landry into slipping up, but she's just a little too good at the spells and charms and whatnot."

"So she spooked you," Slocum said, "and now you want her out of the picture."

"If she took my money to curse Landry, it's only a matter of time before Landry pays her to do the same to me."

"That is, unless she's working for you."

Hal blinked a few times as if those words had literally smacked him in the face. Even after he chewed on his cheroot for a while, the rancher still had to ask, "What did you just say?"

"You heard me right. She could work for you exclusively. I came to an understanding with her while we were locked up and I could arrange it."

"I should just clear out some space in the bunkhouse for a witch? I've heard she sacrifices men to make her potions and fucks others to get certain charms to work. She'd have plenty of chances for both if she was set loose to wander among my men."

"I didn't say a thing about her living here," Slocum pointed out. "All I said was that she'd work for you and not Landry."

Hal's brow furrowed and he shifted the cheroot from one side of his mouth to the other. "Why the hell would I want that?"

"Because she's got Landry afraid of his own barn, half the people in town bite their tongues rather than bring her up in conversation, and the law damn near gives her free rein. That sounds like someone with a whole lot of power if you ask me."

"The sheriff's fixin' to take care of her," Hal carefully pointed out. "You know that better'n anyone."

"Sure, but I've just had a word with Bilson. When it comes to that witch, he doesn't know whether to shoot his pistol or whistle Dixie. He's too worried about answering to a judge if he does anything more than give her a stern warning, and he's too worried about how he looks to the folks in Westlake if he doesn't do anything at all. If you step in and take the problem off his shoulders, Bilson might just wind up in your debt. You think you might be able to put that to some use?"

"You know something?" Hal mused. "I just might."

"That's what I thought. But," Slocum added as he propped his feet upon Hal's desk, "it'll cost you."

13

Slocum rode from the Singer Moon Ranch and headed straight to the Landry spread. Unlike the last time he went there, Slocum wasn't spotted when he approached the front gate of the property. He was spotted long before that.

As the three hired hands fumbled to draw their guns or pull rifles from the boots hanging from their saddles, Slocum kept riding forward. Finally, one of the ranch hands got the guts to speak.

"What the hell do you want?"

"I want to talk to Mr. Landry," Slocum replied.

"Maybe he don't wanna talk to you."

"Maybe you should let him decide that."

The ranch hand shook his head. "He already told us to shoot you dead if you set foot on his land."

Slocum pulled back on his reins to stop within inches of the fence. Ignoring the guns pointed at him, he said, "Then why don't you just ride on back and tell him I got a business proposition for him."

"He won't wanna hear it."

"It's about his witch problem."

Those words sent a visible shudder through all of the armed men on the other side of the fence. Despite the fact that they had their weapons in hand, none of the men seemed comforted by the iron in their grasp.

"Just one of you go then," Slocum offered. "The rest can sit here and keep their guns pointed at me if they like." After saying that, Slocum calmly folded his hands and set them cordially upon his saddle horn.

After a few seconds, the only ranch hand who'd found his voice said, "Fine. I'll go check with Mr. Landry." Looking at the other two, he added, "But only if you hand over your gun first."

"If you want my gun," Slocum growled, "you can come get it for yourself."

"You already killed Paul. We ain't about to let you kill another one of us."

"He forced my hand," Slocum said. "Don't make that same mistake."

All three of the cowboys looked back and forth at one another, nervously waiting for one of the others to make a move. Eventually, the silent two focused their attention on the one who'd done the talking thus far. "We can shoot you right now and there ain't nobody that will know," the spokesman for the three ranch hands stated.

"Really?" Slocum asked. "I'd like to see that."

Finally, the second of the ranch hands got too nervous for his own good. He had a pistol in his hand that was already aimed at Slocum. "To hell with this," he snapped as he thumbed his hammer back.

Slocum acted without hesitation. His hand flashed to the cross-draw holster around his waist and immediately found the Colt Navy. Clearing leather in the blink of an eye, Slocum aimed and fired half a second later. The pistol barked once and knocked the overzealous ranch hand from his saddle like Slocum was shooting a bottle off a fence post. As he fell over, the younger man's finger clenched around his trigger and sent a shot into the air well above Slocum's head.

The horses beneath the remaining ranch hands were obviously more accustomed to rounding up cattle than gunfire, and they responded to the shots by backing away from the fence and threatening to rear up.

As they struggled to regain control of their horses, the ranch hands fired off a few quick shots in Slocum's general direction.

Slocum used an old Indian trick by gripping his saddle horn and leaning sideways until he was hanging off his horse with the animal's thick torso between him and the men that were shooting at him. Although his horse was shifting nervously due to the gunfire, Slocum didn't intend on sacrificing the animal just yet. All he wanted to do was get a bit of cover so he could see what the remaining two cowboys' intentions were.

As if purposely trying to answer Slocum's question, the spokesman for the ranch hands shouted, "Circle around and kill this son of a bitch! One of us will get a clear shot."

Pulling hard on his reins, Slocum brought his horse around in a sharp turn. Soon, he was pointed toward the other two men, who were firing wildly at him. Slocum pulled in a breath, hauled himself back up to sit properly in his saddle, and then let the breath out as he pulled his trigger. When he fired at one of the ranch hands, Slocum knew his aim was true. He was close enough and had a good enough angle that the shot just felt right. Sure enough, the other man cried out and toppled backward from his saddle as blood sprayed from the wound in his chest.

Slocum calmly shifted his aim while the spokesman for the ranch hands levered a fresh round into his rifle and fired it off. The bullet hissed a few inches away from Slocum's shoulder, which didn't affect Slocum's aim in the slightest. His eyes were too focused and his entire body was simply too committed to what he was doing to divert his attention now.

The Colt Navy spat one bullet and then another, causing

the last of the cowboys to do a macabre dance in his saddle. When the lead had finished ripping through him, the ranch hand slouched forward and let his rifle drop. A second later, he followed the rifle to the ground.

As Slocum's eyes took in the land beyond the fence, his hands were busy reloading the Colt. By the time he snapped the cylinder shut, his brow was furrowed in concentration. Before long, that was mixed with a healthy dose of confusion.

Nobody was coming.

Even though there were plenty of acres of land between him and the middle of the property, Slocum guessed that the sound of gunshots would carry for a hell of a long way across all that open country. Even if it didn't make it all the way back to the houses and stables, there had to have been someone else riding the property who'd heard the commotion.

Just to be safe, Slocum gathered up one of the dead men's rifles and prepared to pick off anyone who tried to get a shot at him from afar.

He waited for the better part of a minute without hearing so much as a peep. The only movement he saw was the slow sway of the grass as a breeze made its way to the east.

Suddenly, Slocum got an idea. If he truly had this section of land to himself for the moment, he could do something a hell of a lot better than sit and wait to be found with three more dead Landry men. In fact, he might even be able to add some weight to the case he'd come all this way to make.

Slocum jumped down from his saddle. The bodies were strewn about the ground in a cluster, but he dragged them to create a better formation. Once he was done with that gruesome task, he looked around for any trace that he'd been discovered.

There was still no sign of anyone coming.

Even though he preferred to stay out of the line of fire,

Slocum had to wonder why he'd made such a noisy entrance without anyone else coming to try and chase him off. He'd worked plenty of ranches and knew that gunshots were the best way to catch the attention of partners that were too far away to see. Also, with Landry being so tense on account of the witch, Slocum would have thought security around his place would have gotten tighter rather than slack enough to get away with a gunfight.

That thought led Slocum to the only conclusion that made sense on all counts: Landry's men were busy elsewhere.

Holding out his hands, Slocum approached the only horse that hadn't been spooked by the gunshots. As he walked toward the horse, Slocum made a clucking sound that caused the animal's ears to twitch. Although the horse didn't quite know what to make of Slocum's noises, it didn't run away from him either. Eventually, Slocum got close enough to pat the horse's nose and take hold of its reins.

Slocum led the horse to the fence and kicked out the top rail. He then swatted the horse on the rump, which got it moving toward the fence quickly enough to jump over it once it got there. Slocum ran back to his own horse, pulled himself into the saddle, and rode in the other horse's wake so both sets of tracks mixed together. As long as Landry didn't have a good tracker on his payroll, Slocum was confident his presence was all but erased.

Slocum still wanted to have a word with Landry, but the absence of so many of the rancher's gunmen was nagging at him something fierce. Instead of riding ahead to Landry's house like he'd intended at first, Slocum steered toward Westlake.

Minh's eyes were wide and every muscle in her body was tensed. She had her back to a wall, and was looking at four men who were closer to wild animals than anything human. No matter how frightened she was, she would not allow herself to scream.

"Go on and do it," Coyote growled from behind her as he tightened his grip around Minh's throat. It was difficult to tell whether he was trying to coax a sound from her, or if he was spurring along the man directly in front of her, who had his britches down around his ankles.

The man with his britches down groped at Minh's clothes and started impatiently ripping at the fabric. "I'll do it just as soon as I can get under all of this."

Coyote stood with one shoulder pressed against the wall so he could snarl directly into Minh's ear. "You ain't gonna squeal for me, witch? I bet once I get my turn, you'll be squealing just fine."

Minh strained against Coyote's grip to pull in her next breath. She tried snapping her fist out to defend herself, but that only made Coyote punch her in the back hard enough to send a sharp pain through her entire body. When she tried kicking the man directly in front of her, Minh's knee merely bounced off the young man's tensed stomach.

"You still got some fight in ya," Coyote mused. "Why don't you scream?"

"Maybe witches don't scream," the man in front of Minh said. "But I hear they can do everything else." Sticking his hand between Minh's legs, he grinned and added, "Oh, yeah. You got what I want right there!"

Just then, someone from outside Minh's cabin shouted. That was followed by several shots and then something solid hitting the wall.

Coyote glanced around the little cabin, and then looked over at one of the men near the door. "Go see what that is."

The man at the front of the cabin carried a shotgun, and before he could pull the door open, it was smashed in by a human battering ram. As the body flew through the door and landed on its back, every man except for the one in front of Minh turned to look.

Stepping into the cabin, Slocum extended his arm and shouted, "Minh, get down!"

Although Minh couldn't move far, she turned her head to one side and curled up as best she could. It was enough to clear a path for the bullet that exploded from Slocum's Colt and plowed a nasty hole through the shoulder of the man in front of her. The would-be rapist yelped in pain as he dropped and rolled onto one side. His britches became tangled around his ankles and his erection slapped painfully against the floorboards.

Slocum didn't have to worry about the pair of men that had been posted outside Minh's cabin. He'd dispatched one using a rock to the back of the guy's head, and the other was still recovering after being used to open Minh's front door.

It only took Slocum a second to take in the sight in front of him. Coyote had his back to the farthest wall of the kitchen area and was holding Minh. It didn't take much imagination to figure out the intentions of the man with his pants down. That fellow was still reeling in pain at Minh's feet. A third armed man stood in the corner of the cabin where Minh kept her exotic supplies and mysterious jars. The fellow with the shotgun was closest to the door, and a fifth gunman was near the foot of Minh's bed.

Coyote kept his grip on Minh's neck and pulled her in front of him. "The money on this witch's scalp goes to us!" he said. "You want her, you'll have to fight for her!"

Smiling scornfully, Slocum replied, "That shouldn't be much of a problem."

The man closest to the door may have been shocked by Slocum's entrance, but he'd regained his senses by now. He brought the shotgun up and emptied one of his barrels in a thundering roar that filled the entire cabin.

Slocum dove to one side to avoid being hit. His arm hit the door frame, sending his pistol to the floor, but at least Slocum was able to clear a path for all that buckshot. A section of the door was reduced to splinters as a plume of smoke rolled outside. Before the man holding the shotgun could adjust his aim, Slocum was already driving a fist into his nose. The man's head snapped back as if it was on a spring, so Slocum decided to punch the fellow once more for good measure. That second impact practically turned the man's face into mush.

"Don't just stand there, Abe!" Coyote hollered. "Do something!"

Abe was the man who'd been near Minh's bed. He was quick on his feet, and got to the doorway while Coyote's voice was still cutting through the air.

The man with the busted nose was barely able to see through the tears that had been brought to his eyes, so Slocum had no trouble taking the shotgun away from him. Unfortunately, that man's finger became stuck beneath the trigger guard until it slipped a bit too far in the wrong direction.

The shotgun roared once more and sent its fiery payload into the exotic jars and the man standing near them. Between the buckshot and the flying glass, the gunman in that part of the cabin didn't have a chance. Even though Slocum wasn't caught by the blast, he was close enough to it that his head was immediately filled with a dull roar mixed with a high-pitched ringing. Since the shotgun was empty, Slocum used it to chop Abe's gun hand like an ax, and then swung it back toward its owner's temple, dropping him like a sack of rocks. Although Abe had been forced to drop his pistol, he pulled a hunting knife from a scabbard at his belt and slashed at Slocum's throat.

Leaning back as far as he could while maintaining his balance, Slocum felt a rush of wind as the blade passed by without so much as nicking him. He then raised both arms to block the next swing with the empty shotgun. Abe's arm pounded against the heated iron, stopping the blade less than an inch from Slocum's chest.

For the next few moments, it was a contest of strength between the two men. Abe tried to drive his blade into Slocum's heart while Slocum pushed it back. Slocum took a look over his shoulder to find that the man closest to the door had indeed recovered from the blow to his head. Shifting his weight, Slocum repositioned himself to put Abe off his balance, allowed the shotgun to drop to the floor, and then jumped to one side. As Abe stumbled past him, Slocum grabbed hold of the man's shirt and threw him toward the fellow near the door. The two butted heads like rams, and Slocum was there to take a handful of Abe's hair and slam his head into the other man's face.

Abe staggered away and dropped to one knee, leaving the other one to grab his face and drop against a wall. Slocum squared his shoulders and put his back to a wall so he could focus on the gunmen that remained. Now that those other two were down, he didn't want to give the rest a clear shot at him again.

"Shoot hi—*owwwwwww!!!*" Coyote wailed.

Hearing the command explode into a pained cry caught everyone's attention. Even Slocum had to glance over to the back of the cabin to see what the hell had brought that on. What he found was enough to bring a smile and a wince to his face.

Coyote had been content to watch the fight from the back of the room while issuing orders and maintaining his grip around Minh's throat. Apparently, he'd been neglecting that last part because Minh was able to get her chin down under Coyote's hand so she could sink her teeth into his wrist. Even now, Minh kept biting him until Coyote was in so much pain that he couldn't even make any noise about it.

His mouth hanging open in a silent scream, Coyote tried to pull away from Minh. She wasn't about to let up, however, so she wound up hanging on to the end of his arm with her teeth buried in his flesh. Finally, Coyote tried slamming her against the wall, but only had enough strength to bump her back against the wooden surface.

Minh let go of Coyote's wrist and spat the blood back at him. If anyone in that cabin hadn't had a reason to be scared of her yet, the sight of her standing there with fresh blood dripping from her chin was more than enough to put a fright into anyone. Minh dashed away from Coyote, only to be tripped up by the man on the floor, whose pants were still down and tangled around his legs. She didn't waste a second before cursing at him in her native tongue and driving her foot between his legs.

Already hurting from the gunshot wound, the man on the floor curled up around his aching groin and muttered to himself.

Slocum realized the other men in the cabin had been distracted by Minh's display and were still unable to tear their eyes away from the bloody sight of her.

Rather than try anything fancy, Slocum took advantage of Abe's wandering eye by lowering his shoulder and charging him outright. Abe started to turn toward him, but wasn't able to do anything to avoid catching Slocum's shoulder in his midsection. Soon, both men were headed for one of the broken shelves covered by shattered jars.

Abe kept his feet beneath him, and even got a good hold around one of Slocum's arms. He pounded his fist against Slocum's back, and was just about to hit him again when his back crashed into the shelf.

Slocum could feel Abe's fist on his back for a second before Abe's arms were flung out to either side. Abe let out a strained, wheezing cry and his eyes became wide as dinner plates. Placing a hand on Abe's shoulder, Slocum pulled him forward to find jagged chunks of glass protruding from Abe's back. After he dropped him to the floor, Abe clawed for a few seconds before going limp and letting out one more haggard breath.

"Slocum!"

Recognizing Minh's voice, Slocum turned and rushed to collect his pistol from where it had landed on the floor.

Coyote ran toward the door and jumped through it a fraction of a second before Slocum could pull his trigger. When Slocum got outside, Coyote had a gun in his hand and fired it back at the cabin. Coyote wasn't about to win any marksmanship awards, but he did a hell of a job of getting Slocum to jump back inside and scramble for cover.

"That's right, boy!" Coyote yelled from outside. "Run!"

Slocum gritted his teeth and waited for the shooting to let up so he could take a shot of his own. Beneath all that gunfire, however, Slocum could hear the pounding of boots against the floorboards. Sure enough, when he took a glimpse around the table he'd gotten behind, the only thing he could see was a figure bolting toward the cabin's front door. The shotgunner had gotten his wits about him and was attempting to follow in Coyote's tracks.

"Oh, no, you don't," Slocum growled as he leaned out from behind the table to stop the man any way he could. Before he could get a shot off, Slocum saw his target turn and extend his arm. The instant Slocum caught a glimpse of the gun in the man's hand, he pulled his head back behind the table.

The other man's pistol barked once and punched a hole through the table a few inches shy of Slocum's ear. Still intent on keeping anyone else from escaping, Slocum poked his head out from behind the table. When he discovered that the fleeing man had actually grown a brain in his head and ducked outside, Slocum cursed and jumped away from the table. He rushed to the door and got a quick glimpse outside before being assaulted by a wave of gunfire.

"That's right!" Coyote screamed as he fired again and again at the cabin. "Come on out here!"

Rather than take Coyote up on his invitation, Slocum ran to the closest window and knocked out a corner of glass. Coyote and the other man were both out there, climbing onto their horses while firing wildly at the cabin. By the time Slocum could take a shot at them, both of the two men were snapping their reins and digging their heels into their horses' sides.

Slocum cursed loudly as Coyote and his partner took off in opposite directions. There were too many trees for him to get a clear shot, so Slocum rushed for the door. When he stepped outside, the only trace of those two were the sounds of their horses thundering away from the cabin.

14

Slocum stormed back into the cabin, cursing in a steady growl. His finger itched on his trigger, and he even entertained the notion of firing a few rounds into the men who hadn't made it out of the cabin. Abe lay in a messy pool of blood, the would-be rapist was still curled in a ball, and nearly every piece of furniture was upended. The only thing that had moved since he'd stepped outside was Minh herself.

"Are you all right?" Slocum asked her.

Sitting on her rumpled bed, she nodded.

"What happened?"

"They came about half an hour before you got here," Minh replied.

"Half an hour? Damn it!" Slocum was about to ask what they did in that time, but suddenly thought better of it. From what he'd already seen, those details might not be something she'd want to talk about.

As if reading Slocum's thoughts, Minh said, "They tried talking to me at first. They only started trying to . . ." Lowering her head as well as her voice, she said, "They didn't get a chance to do what they wanted since you showed up."

"What were they talking about?" Slocum asked.

"They asked what I did to curse Landry's ranch. They wanted me to make something to reverse it, and then they wanted me to fix a charm for the ranch instead so they could bring it to their boss and make him pay for it. I took my time mixing something up, but they became impatient."

Slocum reloaded his pistol and dropped it into its place at his side. He then walked over to Minh and sat down on the bed beside her. Although she recoiled at first, she quickly relaxed back into the spot where she'd been. Slocum still didn't try moving any closer.

"Your face is cut," he pointed out as he examined the bloody scrapes on her cheeks and chin. "Did they do that?"

Minh nodded. "When I didn't work fast enough, they hit me. They pushed me around and told me to do what they wanted. I worked faster, but it wasn't fast enough. I thought you would come back soon, so I tried to make them wait as long as I could."

"I'm sorry, Minh. If I knew they'd come for you so soon, I would have—"

"You didn't know," she quickly said. "And you came back. I should be the one who is sorry, John. I thought perhaps you told them to come so you could all claim the reward for my life."

Slocum reached out to gently turn Minh's head so she was facing him. Once she looked into his eyes, he smiled and told her, "There's plenty of reward money out there for both of us."

"Really?"

"Oh, yeah. I had words with the sheriff and Hal Singer just like we discussed. I told the sheriff I could get close enough to kill you, and he offered me a pretty good chunk of change for it. Hal offered me some damn good money to cut a deal with you, and I don't think it should be much of a problem to milk either of them for more."

Minh returned his smile, and was able to keep her chin up without Slocum's help. Scooting to the edge of the bed, she sat perched there with her legs folded beneath her. "Do you think they'll send men after me, too?"

Slocum shook his head. "The sheriff's too squirrelly to send his own men, and he doesn't have the stomach to do it himself. Bilson was plenty happy to have someone step up and take responsibility for the deed on their own, though. I'm sure he wouldn't be reliable enough to back me up once the job's done, but he'd likely pay me under the table."

"You won't need to be backed up," Minh replied. "Especially since you will not truly kill me."

"No, but I'll need something to show him to prove I did in order to get the money. You think you could whip something up for me?"

After thinking for a few seconds, Minh smirked and glanced over at the bodies strewn about the floor. "With their help, I can make something that should convince the sheriff just fine. What about Mr. Singer?"

"He's even easier, since he doesn't want you dead."

"You convinced him I could work for him?"

Slocum smiled and walked over to where the man with his pants down was still huddled on the floor. "It was just as easy as you said it would be."

"I told you so. He made me that offer when he hired me to curse the Landry place. When I refused, he offered me more."

"Well, I told him that I could convince you to rethink that offer. Hopefully, I just might be able to do so."

Slowly, Minh's smile faded. "But that would mean I would have to stay here. That could be unwise if the sheriff is to think I'm dead."

"Not the way I see it," Slocum replied. "All you need to do is whip up a few things for Hal and sign a contract that you'll do more."

"A contract?"

"I know," Slocum chuckled. "It sounds strange, but if Hal's dumb enough to hire a witch and pay through the nose to put her on his payroll, he's dumb enough to draw up a contract to seal the deal. It's just the sort of thing I'd expect from him and to be honest, I'd like to see what kind of nonsense he comes up with. All we need is for him to pay you for signing on and then we're gone."

"We?"

"I'll say I'm seeing to it that you stick to your end of the bargain," Slocum explained. "Truth is, I've had enough of this bullshit and this whole damn town. Hal's paid me well so far, but he owes me for letting me stew in that jailhouse. Hell, he owes me for the goddamn knot on my head from getting bushwhacked by that sheriff. Hal was speaking with that law dog before I was taken in, so he had to have known Bilson was coming for me. Odds are pretty good he handed me over as a way to smooth things out between him, the law, and Landry. That crosses the line, so I'm putting this place behind me and taking a few more of Hal's dollars with me."

"What about Landry?" Minh asked. "Did you talk to him as well?"

"Nope. I had a run-in with some of his men and noticed that the rest of his crew weren't around to come to their rescue. Since Landry doesn't strike me as the sort to turn his hired guns loose and become a man of peace, I figured they were sent somewhere else. I came straight back here to make sure you were accounted for and, well, you know the rest." Reaching down to grab the hair of the man on the floor without any pants, Slocum asked, "Isn't that right?"

All the man could get out was some more pained grunts, so Slocum moved his head up and down.

"Yes," Slocum said. "I thought you knew the rest, because you were right here to see it for yourself. What's your name?"

After pulling in a breath, the man on the floor grunted, "Go to hell."

"That's pretty brave talk coming from a fellow with his

pecker scraping against the floor." Slocum snapped the man's head against the floor and pulled it up again. "What about now? That loosen anything up for you?"

"Jones," the other man said.

"All right, Jones. What brought you all the way down here when nobody's had the sand to come here before?"

"The old man . . . Landry . . . he's put a price on the witch's head."

"Wasn't there one before?"

"Sure, but he doubled it. He even said he struck a deal with the sheriff so's nothin' would happen to anyone that killed her."

Slocum looked over at Minh, but didn't see any sign that she'd been affected by what she'd just heard. He knocked Jones's head against the floor again anyway. "That's no way to treat a lady."

"She's just a damn whore," Jones spat. "I thought I'd take my turn."

Crouching down so he was a bit closer to Jones's level, Slocum tightened his grip on the man's hair and used his other hand to slap the wound on Jones's shoulder as if he was patting him on the back. "I know you're in a bad spot here," Slocum said while Jones squirmed from the rough slaps. "I also know you're trying to keep from looking like any more of an asshole than you already do. Fact of the matter is that there ain't no way for you to look good right about now. And since the only one of your friends still around is him," Slocum added while twisting Jones's head to force him to look at Abe's messy corpse, "there really isn't any reason to keep up the brave act."

"Coyote was the one who rounded us all up," Jones wheezed.

"Keep going."

"None of us wanted to fool with no witch, but Coyote said he could get more money out of Landry. You know . . . just like you was talking about."

Slocum placed his hand on Jones's wounded shoulder and squeezed until Jones curled up into a tight bundle. "See, now I don't want you to spread what I said in here," Slocum calmly stated. "In fact, maybe it was a mistake for me to talk so much." With that, Slocum let go of Jones's hair and drew his pistol. Thumbing back the hammer, he said, "That's a mistake I can fix real quick, though."

"No!" Jones cried. "No, please! I'll do whatever you want. I won't say a word. I swear! Just don't kill me!"

Just then, Slocum couldn't help but notice how Jones curled up to not only protect himself, but also try to cover his naked crotch. The sight would have been funny if it wasn't so pathetic. "Where will Coyote be headed?" Slocum asked.

"Probably into town. He drinks at the Red Diamond Saloon and rents a room there when he's too drunk to make it back to the ranch. He'll go there."

"Not back to Landry's?"

"No. He said we wasn't going back to the ranch until we had that witch's carcass with us. That way, Landry would be locked in to the reward he offered and wouldn't try to get anyone else to come with us. Coyote didn't want to split the money up any more."

"What did you need to bring back to prove she was dead?" Slocum asked.

"Her body or . . . or just her head."

"What about if you brought back—"

"No," Minh snapped.

Slocum and Jones both looked over at her. While they'd been talking, Minh had slipped out of her torn clothes and into a simple brown dress with fringes of different lengths hanging from the seams. There were beads sewn here and there into some sort of pattern, but the dress was so weathered that the design was all but worn away.

"If Landry's fidgety enough to pay through the snout for assholes like these to come after you," Slocum said as he smacked Jones's wounded shoulder one more time, "then he'll accept something other than your head as proof."

"I do not want that pig's money," Minh snarled. "He sends these men after me to put their hands on me and then take my head? Landry will pay for that, but not with money. Besides, the plan must change. If we get too greedy, we may walk away with nothing."

Slocum nodded and then looked back down at Jones. "Ain't she a fine piece of work?"

Jones's eyes were still wide, and only got wider as he watched Minh walk slowly across the room. The instant she so much as glanced in his direction, Jones snapped, "Keep her away from me!"

"Or what?" Slocum asked. "You'll shake yer tallywhacker at us?"

Jones curled up even more and struggled to pull up his pants from that awkward position.

"How many men does Landry have on his payroll?" Slocum asked.

"Counting me, Coyote, and the others that were here . . . maybe a dozen."

Slocum thought back to when he'd paid Landry that first visit. He didn't recall seeing quite that many when he'd shot his way out of there, but there could have been a few doing actual work at the time. "You're sure about that number?"

Having finally tugged his britches up far enough to cover himself, Jones nodded. "More or less. I ain't the one that does the hiring, but there ain't more'n a dozen men about when I'm at the ranch."

"How many are real gunhands?"

"Coyote's a killer, I know that much. A few can handle themselves well enough, and the rest are just cowboys."

Slocum knew most of that already. Since Jones passed his test, Slocum figured it might be worth it to ask one more question. "How far will Landry go to see her dead?"

Jones looked over at Minh, who was gathering up some things that had spilled from her collection of jars. As she worked, Minh stepped over and around Abe's body as if it was a lumpy carpet.

"He wants to be rid of her for good," Jones replied. "I know that much for sure."

"Will he keep sending men after her even if she leaves town?"

Jones blinked as if he'd been given a reprieve. "I . . . I don't think so. If she wants to run, I can go tell Mr. Landry myself! But he'll come after *you*, though. He put up a reward for any of Singer's gunmen that were killed on or off his property."

"Yeah, I already figured that out," Slocum said. "What about Coyote?"

Although Jones averted his eyes rather than answer that question, his fidgeting was all the answer Slocum needed. Coyote wasn't the sort to let Minh go just because she'd outrun him one time. Slocum had seen plenty of men like that and he knew once those kind tasted blood, they went after the rest no matter what. With a reward added to the mix, Coyote would hunt Minh down for a good, long while.

"Tell you what, asshole," Slocum said. "Since you've had a pretty rough night already, I'm gonna give you a chance to save your own skin. I want you to take me to the room that Coyote rents and get him to step outside without a fight. You do that, and I'll consider us square."

Jones was nodding before Slocum had even finished his sentence.

Lunging forward to grab hold of Jones's shirt, Slocum pinned him against the wall. "If there's any more gunmen on Landry's payroll, I want to know about it right now, you hear me?"

"There ain't! I swear! The offer was made to Coyote just a few hours ago. Mr. Landry probably don't even know what happened here!"

"And if you try to double-cross me, I promise you I'll—"

"He won't try to double-cross you," Minh said as she slowly approached the other two.

Suddenly, Jones couldn't stop fidgeting. He twisted and turned against the wall as if he simply no longer worried about the gun in Slocum's hand. "Keep her away from me!"

Slocum glanced at Minh, and saw she was holding a bowl in one hand and a pestle in the other. As she drew closer, she lifted the pestle from the bowl to show some sort of light gray paste dripping from one end.

"What've you got there?" Slocum asked as he started to feel some discomfort of his own.

Minh smiled and kept her eyes locked on Jones. "This is something that will make certain our friend here does what he's supposed to do."

"I'll do whatever you want!" Jones cried.

Slocum had to use almost all of his strength, but he was able to keep Jones more or less pinned against the wall.

"What if he told Mr. Landry I was dead?" Minh said. "That way Landry wouldn't need to send out any more killers for a while."

"Yeah," Slocum said cautiously. "I suppose that would be helpful, but—"

"If Landry learns the truth, we'll already be gone," Minh said as if once again reading Slocum's mind. "In fact, I think it's a wonderful idea." With that, she used the pestle to collect some more of the paste, and then smeared the stuff on Jones's arm.

The moment the pestle made contact with Jones's skin, he kicked and screamed like a newborn baby.

Slocum was barely able to keep hold of the other man, and finally needed to slam Jones against the wall to take some of the fight out of him. "What the hell is that stuff?" he asked.

Minh took the pestle away and held it in front of Jones's face. Once he saw how close the paste was to him, Jones stopped moving and held his breath as if it was his last. "This," she said, "is our way of keeping him in line. You feel how it burns?"

"Y-yes," Jones whimpered.

"What about now? You feel how I can make it burn more?"

Jones was quiet for a few seconds as his eyeballs rattled back and forth within their sockets. After a little while, his eyelids snapped open to their limits and he opened his mouth to let out a bloodcurdling scream. Before he could make so much noise, Slocum slapped a hand over his mouth.

Keeping one hand locked around Jones's arm and his other clamped over the man's mouth, Slocum looked over at Minh. She seemed to be enjoying the show Jones was putting on.

"Now," she said in a vaguely soothing tone, "the burning will not be so bad. I can pull it back so you can understand what we say to you."

Right on cue, Jones eased up on his squirming until he finally stopped altogether. The strain of all that flailing tuckered him out enough for Slocum to keep a better hold on him.

"You will tell Mr. Landry I'm dead," Minh said. "You will tell him I burnt in the fire that was set in this cabin. If he asks for proof, you will tell him it all burnt to ash. If he pays you for my death, you will give the money to someone who deserves it. If you keep any money earned from my death, this burning will scorch all the way down to your bones. Do you understand?"

Jones nodded weakly.

Slocum glanced at the bowl in Minh's hand, but kept his questions to himself. Before Jones could regain his faculties, Slocum slammed him against the wall and snarled, "You won't tell Landry or anyone a goddamn thing about this! If you pass on what you heard here, I'll come back and find you!"

Oddly enough, Jones didn't seem frightened by those words. He seemed somewhat at peace until Minh positioned herself in front of him. Only then did Slocum see the fear return to the man's eyes.

"You wanted to rape me," Minh said.

"I didn't do anything of the sort," Jones protested.

"But you meant to. If things had gone your way, you would have raped me and passed me along to the others. Maybe him," she said as she looked over at Abe's bloody remains.

Jones shook his head, which prompted Slocum to tighten his grip on his shirt and lift him to his tiptoes. "That's bullshit! Why the hell else were your pants down?"

"Take them down again," Minh said.

Both men looked at her and asked, "What?"

Minh nodded. "Take them down. I didn't mix all of this up just to dab on his arm." When she didn't see any movement from Jones, she narrowed her eyes and snapped, "Do it now!"

Jones was trembling like a leaf as he reluctantly pushed his pants down past his waist. When Minh reached out to pull them all the way down, and Slocum kept him from doing anything about it, Jones was fighting back tears.

"Remember what you're supposed to do," Minh said as she moved the pestle around within the bowl. "And remember the burning you're about to feel. If you disobey me, the pain you feel now will be a fond memory in comparison."

With that, Minh moved the pestle between Jones's legs and applied a generous portion of the paste to his crotch.

Even for Slocum, the screams that followed were difficult to stomach.

15

Minh's cabin lit up the entire hillside as it burned. Flames devoured the structure within minutes after Slocum and Minh had set them. Outside, the two of them stood and watched to make certain the fire didn't need any stoking. Even after it became clear there wasn't going to be much left of the cabin, it was difficult for them to take their eyes from the spectacle.

Slocum looked over at her and found Minh gazing at the blaze as if it was some kind of dream. "We should get moving," he said. "Someone's bound to see this fire before too long."

She nodded, and stooped to gather some of the bags at her feet. "They will see it, but they won't come," she said quietly. Having collected as much as she could before the fire had gotten started, she wound up with four heavy carpet-bags that had been stitched up with hunks of burlap. Two of them had typical handles, while another two had additional leather straps.

"Need any help with those?" Slocum asked.

"No," she replied as she hung the two bags with straps over her shoulders. "Someone should never travel with more than they can carry."

Slocum chuckled, and picked up one of the remaining bags anyway. "I know plenty of women who haven't learned that lesson. Even so, I might as well be of some use."

Minh climbed into her saddle and hung one of the bags from its horn. She left the other two hanging from her shoulders with the straps crossing her torso like bandoliers. "You saved my life," she replied.

"Just barely. I was too late to stop them bastards from beating you."

"I've had worse. You arrived before it became much worse."

"No woman should have to take that. As for those men, well, any man who rapes a woman ain't nothing but an animal and those kinds of animals get put down before they hurt anyone else. Speaking of them kinds of men," Slocum added as he glanced down the trail that led from the cabin and into Westlake, "what in blazes was that stuff you put on Jones?"

Minh smirked as she looked down that same path. Not too long ago, they'd turned Jones loose so he could run down that road. He'd done so as if his tail was burning brighter than the cabin, and he hadn't stopped until he was well out of sight. Finally, she told Slocum, "Ginger, some hot peppers, a dab of snake venom, some poison oak, as well as a few other things."

"The way he was carrying on, I'd say he was doing a lot more than itching."

"I also ground up some thorns, wasp stingers, scorpion tails, and little pieces of broken glass. You can't grind those up too much, though," she added as if she was sharing a recipe for pumpkin pie. "They've got to blend in with the paste, but really get under the skin as he scratches it in. If I do it just right, some of the bits actually stay with him for days or even weeks.

"It's a mixture I made up myself," she continued. "It burns at first, until the glass and stingers settle under the skin. Once the spices and venom get into the blood, the burning comes and goes. I tell him I control the burning myself and he doesn't know the difference."

"Will it last long enough to get the job done?"

"Oh, yes," Minh said. "What I put on him might stretch it out for a week. Just when he thinks he is free, he will move just the right way and get it going all over again. If he tries to scrub it off, well, that will make it much worse. He'll think I'm toying with him."

Thinking back to where the paste had been applied and how well Minh had ground it into his flesh using the pestle, Slocum winced and let out a whistle. "Damn. Maybe it would have been easier just to shoot the son of a bitch."

"Easier, but not so gratifying."

They laughed for a bit as they rode away from the burning cabin. Where the road curved toward Westlake, Slocum and Minh turned in the opposite direction so the town was behind them. Before they got too far, Minh stuck her hand into one of the bags strapped across her chest and pulled out something that Slocum recognized right away.

"Is that what I think it is?" he asked.

She stretched her arm out to hand him the tangled mess of hair she was holding. Nodding, she replied, "It's a scalp. It belonged to one of the men who tried to kill me."

"The one whose head you put on a pike?"

"No. A different one."

Slocum might have had his doubts regarding Minh's stories, but the scalp she was holding lent some credence to them. She could still be stretching the truth to maintain her standing as a witch, and might have gotten that scalp from any number of unscrupulous traders who'd been through Indian country. Rather than ask too many questions, Slocum took the grisly keepsake and looked it over.

"I suppose this could be yours," he admitted. "Not that many folks have gotten a close enough look to know the difference."

"You've seen me more than anyone in town has ever cared to."

"Well, that's their loss."

For the first time in a while, Minh allowed herself to relax a bit and smile warmly. Unlike the nervous laughter they'd shared a few moments ago, this truly took away some of the fire in her eyes and gave Slocum a glimpse of the woman instead of the witch. "Thank you, John," she said. "I owe you so much. But why have you gone through so much trouble?"

"I don't believe in witches, remember?"

"But you could have been killed back there."

"It's like I already said. No woman deserves what was about to happen to you in that cabin. And there's still money to be made, unless you've forgotten."

"I know, but . . . never mind. I suppose I'm just not used to anyone showing me so much kindness."

"If it's kindness you want," Slocum said, "you might want to stop cursing folks."

She shrugged, and turned so she was facing the rough little path that cut across some tough terrain before meeting up with the main trail leading to the Singer Moon Ranch. "I need to make money and I never learned to sew."

The answer was quick and to the point. It stunned Slocum for a moment, before he broke out in a laugh that stuck with him all the way to the fence line.

Slocum knew Hal's land well enough to get past the men guarding the herd and up to the Singer family home. Having tied up her horse a short distance off Hal's property, Minh rode with Slocum with her face covered and her arms wrapped around his midsection. When they got to the house, it was late enough that there was only one man in the area to spot them.

Robbie approached Slocum with a rifle resting over his shoulder in a lazy grip. "That you again, Slocum?" he asked.

"Sure is."

"Who's that with you?"

"Someone Hal wanted to see." Between the bandanna tied around her face and the oversized hat on her head, there wasn't much of a chance that anyone could recognize her. Slocum didn't own enough bandannas, however, to cover up Minh's slender, attractive curves. Leaning in to Robbie and dropping his voice to a whisper, Slocum added, "She's from town and Hal won't want the wife or anyone else to know about her. Get me?"

After glancing between Slocum and Minh a few times, Robbie finally nodded. "Oh, you mean she's—" He dropped his voice to a whisper as well and asked, "She's one of *those* ladies from town?"

"That's right and she's only paid up through the night, so Hal won't want me to dawdle before bringing her to him."

Robbie backed up and raised his eyebrows. Surely, the ranch hand was thinking about how he could spread this new bit of gossip, but that wasn't Slocum's concern. After getting Minh to the house, he had to get her into the rancher's office without causing a fuss. Fortunately, the only light inside the house was in Hal's office. A few lanterns burned in there, casting a fretful shadow that paced back and forth in front of the office door. Slocum led Minh in that direction, and almost made it before Hal knew he was there.

Almost, but not quite.

Hal stomped toward the door and stuck his head out. "What the hell? Slocum?"

Nodding as he walked down the short hallway, Slocum replied, "I said I'd come back, didn't I?"

"Yeah, but it's damn late. How'd you get in here anyway?"

"I think this one should take credit for that." Stepping aside, Slocum gave Minh some space so she could present herself. She removed her hat, pulled down the bandanna that had been covering her face, and looked calmly at the rancher.

Hal sputtered for a few seconds before motioning for them to come closer. "Get in here," he said. "No need waking everyone up."

"Is someone here?" Kelly called down from upstairs.

"Go back to sleep!" Hal bellowed. With that, he slammed his office door shut.

If the entire ranch wasn't so accustomed to Hal's big mouth, more would have been made over the commotion. As it was, whoever heard the ruckus would merely shrug and go back to bed for the night.

Standing with his back against the office door as if he was repelling an invasion force, Hal snapped, "What is she doing here?"

"We talked about this, Hal," Slocum replied. "You said you'd pay to get her working for you exclusively. Here she is."

"Yes, but things are awfully hot right now. What am I supposed to do with her until they cool down?" Hal stammered.

Slocum shrugged. "That's up to you. I brought her here to make the agreement, so where's my money?" Narrowing his eyes, Slocum added, "And don't tell me it's at the bank. I don't have the time to fool about with that."

"Why not?" Hal asked nervously. "Got somewhere better to be?"

"As a matter of fact I do. This is my last job for you," Slocum told him. "Whatever you owe needs to be paid up right now."

"And," Minh added, "I suggest you pay in full."

Those words from her seemed to carry more weight than everything else Slocum had said up to that point. Hal scurried around his desk and pulled open a drawer to remove an iron lockbox. Fishing out a key that hung from a chain around his neck, he unlocked the box and removed a handful of cash from inside.

"Was that always there?" Slocum asked. "Even when you made me go all the way to the damn bank?"

"Of course not, Slocum," Hal nervously replied. "That is, I had to make sure that it was—"

"Aw, forget it," Slocum grumbled. "Just get me my damn money."

Hal counted out everything Slocum was owed, including the fee for getting Minh to agree to their proposal. When he handed over that last sum, Hal seemed to have an especially hard time letting it go.

"Truth be told," the rancher said sheepishly, "I didn't expect you to pull this off."

"Yeah," Slocum said as he took the money. "I guessed as much."

Shifting his eyes to Minh, Hal asked, "So will you be able to keep that curse hanging over Landry's head for a while?"

She nodded solemnly.

"And will you pay him a visit to make certain he's doubly spooked? The more nervous Landry is, the sloppier he gets."

"When I visit him," Minh said, "he will fear for his life."

"Really?"

"Yes. For after this night, everyone will think I'm dead."

Hal's eyes widened and he looked over to Slocum.

"It's true," Slocum said. "Her house is burning as we speak. Needless to say, it'd be best for you to keep this visit under your hat."

Nodding anxiously, Hal closed up his lockbox and put it back in the drawer. After that, he slapped his hands together and rubbed them with enough enthusiasm to start a fire of his own. "Better yet, I can spread all kinds of stories. Stories about your ghost and how I've seen it around. I can have my men spread it, too, in all the saloons and such until this whole town's lookin' over their shoulders. Then, when those curses keep happening, I bet ol' Landry will swear he's seen your ghost, too. This will be the most fun I've had in years!"

"Say nothing about seeing me after the fire," Minh warned. "Other than that, you can say what you will."

"Sure," Hal said quickly. "What kind of fee do you want for the curse?"

"I will take a small amount now and the rest in a month. After that, you can pay me every month for as long as you want my services to continue."

"All right then. How's about three hundred for an advance on the first month?"

Minh narrowed her eyes a bit more until they were slits.

"Three-fifty," Hal quickly amended. "But not another penny more until I see some results."

Nodding, Minh said, "That will be fine."

Hal collected the money and handed it over. Oddly enough, when Slocum and Minh left his office, the rancher was the one smiling.

Slocum walked up to Sheriff Bilson's office alone. He was spotted by a deputy, who promptly started to question him, but Slocum ignored the younger lawman and headed straight for the senior town official. When Slocum stormed into the office, he found Bilson at his desk. The sheriff was asleep, but woke up quickly enough once the door slammed shut.

Snapping his head up, Bilson nearly fell over backward in his haste to swing his feet off his desk. It took a few seconds for him to catch his breath and collect himself. The lawman's composure lasted right until Slocum tossed the scalp down in front of him.

"There," Slocum said. "The witch is dead."

"Wha?" Still groggy, Bilson started to pick up the scalp. He let it drop the moment he realized what it was. "Is that . . . is that fresh?"

"It's a little dried out, but that's because of the fire."

"The fire. Oh, right. One of my boys told me about that.

There ain't nothing to do but let the place burn. You saying that witch was in there?"

Slocum nodded. "All but that piece of her. That's as good as I could do before getting burned up myself. Sorry about the rough edges."

The more Slocum talked about the scalp, the less Bilson wanted to look at it. "Well, since shots were heard comin' from that place, I suppose there's no reason to doubt you. Seein' as how there ain't no body, though, I'd say only half the reward is due."

"Half, huh?" After thinking it over for all of two seconds, Slocum grabbed the scalp and shook his head. "Nah. I'm sure I can get plenty more for a genuine witch's scalp. They might even feel sorry for me once I tell them how you bilked me out of the rest of this bounty."

Sheriff Bilson leapt to his feet. "Not a bounty! Officially, I didn't offer any such thing. Not for some damned witch!" As if thinking he was under a magnifying glass, Bilson lowered his voice and added, "The point of getting rid of her was to make things easier around here. Spreadin' them lies will just—"

"It'll make things harder for you maybe," Slocum interrupted. "That is, only if you had aspirations to advance in an upstanding career. Oh, wait, you did have aspirations, didn't you?"

"Fine, you'll get the whole reward. Come back tomorrow for it."

"Nope. You must keep funds about to pay off bounties and such. What about the money collected for fines or—"

"It ain't a bounty," Bilson hissed. Stomping across the room to a locked gun cabinet, Bilson unlocked it and then unlocked another compartment within the cabinet, which contained a small stash of money. "Here," he said as he handed the money over. "It's all I got. You want the rest, you'll have to come back tomorrow."

Slocum riffled through the money and took a quick

count. There was close to a thousand there. Looking up, he asked, "You really keep so much on hand for bounties?"

"If you must know, that was money to build a new jailhouse."

Considering that the town had been abuzz with talk of the new jailhouse the day Slocum first arrived to get work at the Singer Moon, and not a lick of building had been done in the time that followed, he didn't feel too bad for taking the money. Bilson was probably just sitting on it until the town forgot about the groundbreaking anyway.

Slocum touched the money to the brim of his hat and smirked. "Pleasure doin' business with you, Sheriff. Far as I'm concerned, this here money is payment for a job well done. No bounty here."

"Get out and leave me in peace."

"Sure thing. Keep up the fine job." When he said that last part, Slocum didn't even try to sound earnest.

As Slocum rode to the dry riverbed outside of town, he was whistling a happy little tune. He didn't know the name of the river or when it had dried up, but he knew that Minh was supposed to be waiting for him there and they would finally be leaving Westlake. He didn't see her at first, but it was so dark that he couldn't see much of anything but the ground under him. Slocum brought his horse to a stop and kept whistling.

Before too long, a shape emerged from the shadows to come up beside him.

"You sound happy," Minh said as she pulled back on her reins and looked over at him. "Does that mean things went well?"

Slocum took a bundle of cash from his pocket and handed it to her. "Judge for yourself. I still say we could have gotten some more out of Hal if we'd pressed him."

Minh ran her fingers along the edge of the bundled money and smiled. "We got plenty. Considering this is all pay for jobs that weren't done, we should be happy with anything at all."

"A witch with a conscience, huh? I like that."

Although Minh scowled at first, she quickly shrugged after considering the source of the snide remark.

"And don't feel too bad about taking this money," Slocum continued. "It comes from men that wanted to use you or see you dead. If I were you, I wouldn't lose a wink of sleep over it. Also, the jobs are getting done."

"How do you figure that?"

"Well, the sheriff wanted you out of his hair and you will be. Hal wanted something to ruffle Landry's feathers and he's got it."

"But Landry thinks I am dead," Minh pointed out. "The man I sent to relay that news will do what he is told."

"If a man believes in witches, he'll believe in ghosts. I'm sure Hal will think of something to keep Landry on his toes for a while. He only paid for a month anyhow, so you don't have to come back."

Minh nodded and glanced in the direction of Westlake. "I suppose you are right. Still, that was my home and I was settled there. Most of those people may have been scared of me a little, but they came to me anyway for help with little things. I helped them and it was nice. I can come back every now and then. Perhaps when the moon is full."

For a second, Slocum couldn't tell whether or not Minh was joking. But even in the darkness, he could see the genuine sorrow in her eyes. "I suppose you did have a good thing going there," Slocum admitted. "But it ran its course. Haven't you had to pick up and move before?"

"Yes." Shifting to face the road ahead, she straightened up and added, "I will move on and start again. Truman's Crossing should be a good place for that."

"It's a few days ride from here, but are you sure it's far enough? I mean, stories of the witch of Westlake might have spread far and wide."

"Those stories don't travel as far as you may think," Minh told him. "Ackerville is only thirty miles north, and I can go there freely without being known as anyone but just another woman mistaken as Chinese. We will know soon enough if Truman's Crossing will be safe once we get there. Are you certain you wish to go with me?"

"Sure," Slocum replied. "It was my idea to wring some traveling money from those folks, so I might as well stay with you to make certain nobody comes after it."

"You are a good man, John."

Snapping his reins, Slocum waited for Minh to match his pace before telling her, "Give it a little while. You'll be happy to be rid of me soon enough."

Two men lay on their bellies behind some bushes no more than fifteen yards from where Slocum and Minh had been talking. One of them lifted his head up once Slocum led the way from the riverbed, and then turned to show an ugly smile to the second man. "I'll be damned," Coyote said. "You were right. Get the horses and we can follow 'em."

Brady propped himself up using his arms, and winced as the movement pulled on the stitches in his side. "Give 'em some breathing room. Me and the kid have been keepin' track of that asshole since Mr. Landry got us set loose from jail. We can follow 'em a bit longer."

16

It was a short ride to Ackerville, but Slocum and Minh took
their time getting there. They rode north from Westlake,
picked a spot to camp about half a mile outside Ackerville,
and took turns watching for a posse made up of lawmen or
angry ranch hands. Since neither group showed up, Slocum
cooked up a simple breakfast of beans and bacon while
Minh ground up something in one of her bowls.

"What's that?" Slocum asked as he divided the beans
between them. "Some concoction for making the horses
run faster? A powder to sprinkle on the road to keep our
tracks from being seen?"

"It's a kind of oatmeal that my mother used to make," she
replied simply. "I thought it would go well with the bacon."

Slocum chuckled, and leaned over to get a better look at
the bowl. "Oh. It does smell awfully good."

"Tastes even better."

Despite all his talk about how witchcraft was nonsense
and folks were foolish to believe in those sorts of things,
Slocum had to admit he'd started believing some of them
himself. He'd seen the things Minh had done, and had even
gotten a glimpse of how she'd gotten her tricks to work.
Her charms wound up having fairly simple mechanics be-

hind them, and her potions were merely strange recipes using regular things. Even so, he felt a reluctant twinge in his belly when he dipped a spoon into her bowl to sample her oatmeal.

It turned out she was right. It did taste pretty good.

They finished their meal and quietly enjoyed the early morning. After collecting their things, they rode into Ackerville and bought some supplies. Slocum's first instinct was to wrap up Minh good and tight so her face wouldn't be seen. Then he decided to put her previous theory to the test and see if the witch stories truly hadn't spread too far from Westlake.

Once in Ackerville, they walked into the first general store they could find just like any other pair of folks who needed some things for a long ride. Minh dressed in her normal buckskins, but wore a large scarf tied around her waist like a makeshift skirt. A matching bandanna was tied around her neck, and her hat hung off her head against her back.

"You folks just passing through?" the clerk asked. He was a tall fellow with tousled gray hair and a pair of round spectacles perched on the bridge of his nose. His smile was amicable but cautious.

Slocum piled up the supplies he'd collected and nodded. "That's right. We're on our way to Westlake."

Immediately, the clerk frowned. "Oh, I've heard some things about that place."

"Really? What have you heard?"

"There's been some trouble there lately. Something about men getting shot as part of some sort of feud between two ranchers there. Nasty business."

"Is that all?" Slocum asked.

Pausing in the middle of scribbling prices onto a piece of paper, the clerk furrowed his brow and looked up as though a report was pasted to the ceiling. "All that I know of," he finally said before getting back to figuring up the total.

As if to prove the point she'd made earlier, Minh looked directly at the clerk and said, "I have heard stories about a witch there. Is that true?"

The clerk chuckled and replied, "I've heard something about that, too, but I wouldn't let it get to you none. One of the hotels right here in Ackerville is said to be haunted by demons that rattle the windows and push all the dishes about. It's probably just guests making a ruckus and loose boards. The witch of Westlake is probably just some poor old woman who gets teased by the children. This'll be three dollars and twenty-eight cents."

As Slocum counted out the money to pay for the supplies, he looked over at Minh and wasn't surprised to find her grinning back at him. When she didn't say anything else, he guessed he was in the clear. She remained quiet while the clerk went through some more small talk and then bundled up the supplies. Even when they loaded the things onto the horses and climbed into the saddles, she kept to herself. It wasn't until they were riding out of Ackerville that she looked over at him and said the four words Slocum had been expecting the entire time.

"I told you so."

Slocum nodded and kept his mouth shut. There was still plenty of ground to cover between Ackerville and Truman's Crossing, and he didn't want to make the trip with an angry witch.

Truman's Crossing was roughly the same size as Westlake. There weren't quite as many saloons or whorehouses, simply because there were fewer ranches in the immediate area. That meant fewer cowboys and deeper roots beneath the folks who lived there. Since they didn't cater to the wilder crowd, the locals were quieter and set in their ways. No less than three churches were scattered within the town, and banners were strung across their main streets advertising some sort of gala quilting contest or a similar event.

Slocum didn't give those banners much thought, since he was too busy looking for a good saloon.

While there may not have been entire sections of the town devoted to whiskey and women, Slocum was able to find a place that served both to their customers. The whiskey was of higher quality and the women simply kept their business off the streets where the kids and upstanding citizens could see. The town was a bit too quiet for him, but Minh seemed to like it just fine. Even after their first couple of weeks there, Slocum was still surprised to hear her say that.

"You really like it here?" he asked.

Minh nodded, and arranged her newly bought jars on the shelves that had just been built in the corner of her new home. It was a little house on the outskirts of town and was slightly bigger than the cabin she'd once had. Already, it was starting to feel a lot like that old place. "This is a nice town," she replied. "Why wouldn't I like it?"

Walking over to a window, Slocum pulled back a curtain and looked outside. It was early evening, but the streets were already empty. "I don't know. It's just a bit too quiet for my tastes."

"Then leave."

"You getting sick of me?"

"No," she replied as she straightened a row of jars that were filled with something that was bright yellow and pickled. "I don't need you to look in on me. You want to leave, so leave. You must be getting tired of sleeping in that room over the saloon."

"Actually, I been sleeping in the stall with my horse. It's cheaper."

"You already spent all that money?"

"No. Just saving it. I see you've probably spent all of yours on this house and such."

"I am making money already. There are women in town who want good-luck charms for the quilting contest. A few have daughters who want to find a husband. Tomorrow, I see a man who wants me to bless his new store. That is how my business starts."

"I wouldn't have pegged churchgoing folks as the sort who would visit a witch."

"Church people are the most superstitious of anyone. And besides, nobody calls me a witch. They just buy some of my spices and then a few good-luck charms."

"I guess I just don't know all the finer points of witchcraft," Slocum admitted.

"No. You do not." With that, Minh finished what she was doing and then turned toward Slocum. "There has been some talk about what other valuables I may have besides my spices. When people talk about what they see in here, they start to wonder what other things I may be hiding. They look at my mother's old teapots and think they are valuable antiques. Some of them are. Some people will eventually get the idea to try and take them from me."

"Only been a few weeks and already getting suspicious about everyone, huh?"

Minh smiled and approached him. "I can only sell good-luck charms for so long. I need to plant the seeds that I am more than a strange lady who can get rare spices. When they start to think I can do charms as well as curses and other magical things, they will come to me more."

"And pay you more," Slocum said.

"That's right."

"So what do you want from me? Should I keep my eyes open for anyone sneaking around here looking to steal from you?"

She shook her head and gazed into his eyes. "No. I won't let things here go as far as they did in Westlake. I can protect myself from troublemakers and thieves without frightening the whole town. You have done so much and I wanted to make sure I thanked you for everything."

Slocum patted the pocket where he kept most of his

money and said, "No need to thank me. Everyone back at
Westlake thanked me plenty already."

"But they cannot thank you the way I can," Minh said as
she stepped even closer to him and placed her lips upon his
mouth. She kissed him lightly at first, but soon she was hungrily chewing on his lip and using both hands to eagerly un-
dress him.

"Now that," Slocum said as he shrugged out of his shirt
and let her peel it off him, "is the kind of payment I will
accept."

Minh pulled at his belt until she nearly ripped the buckle
off. After that, she unfastened his pants and tugged them
down while dropping to her knees in front of him. Within
seconds, she had his cock in her hands and was stroking it
slowly. As soon as he began to grow hard, she opened her
mouth and took him inside. Minh's lips slid against his sen-
sitive skin and her tongue grazed along the bottom of his
shaft until he was almost fully erect.

Slocum took off the rest of his clothes and then looked
down at her. Minh looked right back up at him while sliding her mouth back and forth along his length. She even
reached out to scrape her hands along his chest as she devoured every last inch of him and held him in her throat for
a few seconds. When she leaned back, she let him fall from
her mouth and resumed stroking him with her hand. "Lay
down," she told him.

Slocum took a few backward steps toward the bed before he was guided by Minh's hands upon his chest. She
pushed him in the right direction, and when he finally let
himself drop onto the bed, Slocum was treated to a nice
show. Minh eased out of her clothes while rarely letting her
hands stray from her own body. She kept moving her hands
along her bare skin, savoring every bit of it.

Climbing onto the bed, she closed her eyes and leaned
back. Minh eased one hand along the flat surface of her
belly and down to the thatch of dark hair between her legs

as her other hand moved up between her little breasts. By the time her hand reached the base of her neck, both nipples were fully erect and she was swaying gently from side to side.

As Slocum lay there and watched, he could feel his entire body start to ache for her. Seeing her tight little form so close was almost too much for him to bear. Before he gave in and grabbed hold of her, Minh shifted her attentions back to him and lowered her mouth down onto his stiff member.

She wrapped her lips around his cock and sucked while her tongue swirled around the tip and her hands moved between his thighs. When she felt Slocum's hands on her, she moved so she was lying on top of him and her hips were directly over his face.

Slocum reached up with both hands to rub Minh's tight little ass. Her pussy was directly over his mouth, and all he had to do was lift his head a bit to get a good taste of her. She was every bit as sweet as she looked. The pink lips between her legs glistened with moisture, and her entire body shuddered when he ran his tongue up and down along them. All he had to do was touch her clitoris with his mouth to get her trembling even harder.

Minh sat up and supported her weight on her knees so she could keep her pussy just above Slocum's mouth. She placed her hands flat on his stomach and arched her back as his mouth worked its magic on her. Before too long, she turned around and straddled his chest so she could look down at his face. As Slocum watched, she ran her hands up and down along her body. She cupped her little breasts and played with her nipples before running her fingertips all the way down to her thighs. Before her fingers could make the return trip back up, Slocum grabbed her wrists and pulled her down so he could taste her some more.

First, he sampled the smooth skin of her stomach. As she moved her hips down toward his hard cock, Slocum ran his tongue up between her breasts to taste her there. She didn't taste like just any woman. In fact, there was something else on her skin that reminded him of all the spices and herbs she used for her concoctions. As he'd spent time with her over the last few weeks in Truman's Crossing, he'd become more acquainted with that scent. Now that he was tasting it on her skin, it made his mouth warm.

When she'd positioned herself so her face was above his, Slocum tried to kiss her. Minh responded by sitting upright and reaching down to guide him between her legs. The next thing Slocum felt was the tight grip of her pussy as she took him inside and eased herself down onto him. Minh placed her hands flat on Slocum's stomach and wriggled her hips in a rhythm that took them back and forth faster and faster. Before she could bring him too far too fast, Slocum sat up with the intention of laying Minh on her back so he could pound into her. Before he could do that, however, she curled her legs around him and locked her hands behind his neck.

Slocum felt tangled up for a moment, but that quickly faded once Minh began pumping her hips back and forth. They sat upright, facing each other with their legs wrapped around each other and looking directly into each other's eyes. Since he was still inside her, Slocum could thrust in and out of her to his heart's content. In fact, once Minh leaned back a little, he was able to pound into her with enough force to shake the bed.

She clenched her eyes shut and turned her head while letting out a prolonged moan. Soon, she spread her knees apart farther to give Slocum free rein between them. He drove into her a few times until both of their bodies were grinding against each other.

Minh tightened her fists around bunches of her blanket as a powerful orgasm swept through her. Slocum wasn't far behind, and after thrusting his hips forward one more time, he exploded inside her.

Slowly, Minh eased away from him until his cock slipped

out of her. She moved her hand over it, and then eased it back up to the moist lips between her thighs. She kept her eyes open and locked on him as she rubbed tiny circles around her clitoris for the few moments it took to get her trembling with pleasure one more time.

Even though Slocum only had to sit back and watch her, he felt just as good as when she'd been wrapped around him. When she started to moan again, he felt his body respond to it. He grew hard, which she spotted immediately. Still sitting directly across from him on the bed, Minh reached out to stroke his member.

Slocum wanted to get back inside her, but her hand moved so well on him that he barely had the strength to prop himself up. "That's enough," he said as he lay back. "At least, for now. Just . . . let me catch my breath."

"Are you all right?" she asked.

"Yeah, just need a bit to collect myself." As he said that, Slocum felt fatigue creeping in on him from all sides. Considering what he'd been doing, he wasn't too surprised by that. What he didn't expect, however, was to feel the room start to wobble beneath him. When he lifted his head, he felt as though the entire house was spinning.

"You don't look so good," Minh said.

"I feel . . ." Slocum was going to say he felt fine. A little tired, but fine. With every second that ticked by, he wondered just how fine he was. And, as more seconds passed, he knew he wasn't fine at all. "Help me up," he said.

After hopping off the bed, Minh rushed around to slip her hands beneath Slocum's shoulders and around the back of his neck. She was able to lift him up halfway, but when he began to fall back down again, she strained to keep him there. "You need to sit up," she urged.

"I'm trying, damn it! Something's . . ."

Slocum couldn't recall saying much after that. He knew he was talking, but he couldn't hear the words that were coming out of his mouth. He knew he was moving, but it felt more like flailing at the bottom of a deep, cold lake.

With Minh's help, he was barely able to get to his feet.

She placed something on his tongue, which helped clear his head a bit.

"Come . . . me," Minh said through the fog that grew thicker and thicker within Slocum's head. ". . . going . . . see the doctor."

17

There were plenty of noises drifting through Slocum's ears, but he couldn't distinguish the voices from the rattle of wagon wheels. He guessed he was outside, but he didn't even recall leaving Minh's house. He hoped he was dressed, and he prayed he wasn't stumbling into the street where he would get trampled by a horse.

"John, wake up!"

It sounded like Minh's voice, but Slocum couldn't be certain. Suddenly, he got a strong taste of something sharply bitter that opened his eyes and brought things into a bit more focus. He was outside. He wasn't in the street. Minh was helping him walk along the boardwalk of Second Street, which cut through a quiet section of Truman's Crossing. Before he could take in much more than that, Slocum's face was roughly turned to one side.

"Can you hear me?" Minh asked as she forced Slocum to look at her. "You've got to wake up!"

"What? Why?"

Keeping hold of Slocum's chin, she twisted his head toward the street and held it there. "Look. Do you see them?"

Slocum saw them all right. It took a moment for him to recall the names through the haze in his skull, but he recognized the ugly face of the man who walked a few steps ahead of the other two men behind him.

"Well, well," Coyote said through a wide, toothy grin. "Looks like you're a little out of sorts, boy."

Pulling himself up to stand as straight as he could, Slocum said, "Last time I saw you, you was running like a scalded dog. What brings you back?"

Coyote squinted and planted his feet on the boardwalk about ten paces in front of Slocum. The other two men stopped on either side of him. "You're slurring yer words there," Coyote said. "Are you drunk?"

One of the men with Coyote leaned forward and studied Slocum. "He looks a little green behind the ears to me. I don't think he feels too good."

"Brady," Slocum said. He then nodded as the name sank in. "Hal's men were to hand you over to the law and I didn't hear any different, so that means someone must'a gotten you out." He blinked a few times as his senses came back to him. Although Slocum was able to stand without so much help from Minh, he still wasn't about to do a jig. "Landry was the one who hired you to steal them cattle. He's also on good terms with Sheriff Bilson, so he's got to be the one who got you set loose."

Brady nodded slowly and tipped his hat. Motioning to the man on the other side of Coyote, he said, "Me and the kid both got out. We even got patched up in time to ride out for one more job. We meant to tell Landry to stuff his job up his ass, but when we heard Coyote was gonna track you and that witch down, we couldn't pass up the opportunity."

"Yeah," the kid snapped. "Nobody gets to toss us around like you did without payin' for it!"

"Shut up, kid," Brady said with barely a nod in the younger gunman's direction. "Let's take care of this quick."

Slocum let his hand drop to his side, and was relieved to feel it graze against the Colt Navy holstered there. The moment he felt the familiar weight on his hip, Slocum recalled buckling the gun belt around his waist before having set foot outside. The action was as much a reflex to him as scratching his nose. "It's been weeks since we left West-lake," Slocum said as he fought to clear what felt like mist behind his eyes. "What the hell are you doing here?"

"Landry's still offering a price on her head," Coyote replied as he leveled a finger at Minh. "He knows she weren't dead because I know she was still breathin' when I left that cabin."

"Ran from the cabin is more like it," Slocum corrected.

Coyote nodded. "I only ran so's I could watch and see where you went after the smoke cleared. You didn't have the first notion I was behind you, even after Mr. Landry sent these two to back my play. We thought we'd wait for you to leave before pickin' her off, but this looks like one hell of a good opportunity to put you in yer place as well."

Slocum pulled in a deep breath, trying his damnedest to look like he had all his wits about him. "You mean since I look like easy pickings?"

"You can call it what you like," Brady said. "Since you couldn't do much of anything to me or the kid without us bein' tied up first, you ain't got no room to talk."

"You men are too yellow to do anything out in the open," Slocum said. "Otherwise, you wouldn't have stepped up now that I look like I'm sick as a dog. Come on, Minh. Let's keep walking and I'm sure this trash won't follow us much longer."

Minh stepped up close to him and placed her mouth against Slocum's ear. "You must deal with them now. If you wait, you will only feel worse."

"Huh?"

But Slocum didn't need her to answer his grunt of a question. Just pushing that word out felt as if he was about to push out everything in his stomach right along with it. He might not know what the hell was wrong with him, but

Slocum had drunk enough whiskey in his day to know when he was about to be sick in a messy way. The vomit rose up toward the back of his throat, and wouldn't be held at bay for much longer.

Sucking in enough air to fill his lungs, Slocum pushed Minh aside and stood on his own two feet. He looked around to find a few people about, but no more than three or four along the street. As far as he could tell by the silence in the air and the darkness of the sky, it had to be getting close to midnight.

"You men followed us all the way from Westlake to collect on some reward?" Slocum asked.

"Me an' the kid will shoot you dead for free," Brady replied.

Slocum held out his left hand and motioned them forward. "All right then. Make your move or get the hell out of my sight. As for you," he added while pointing at Coyote. "You can scamper away like a good little doggie any time you like."

The smug grin on Brady's face showed a bit of tarnish now that Slocum was standing on his own steam.

The kid looked jittery as always.

Coyote gritted his teeth in a snarl that would do his namesake proud. "He can't take all of us at once," he said. And before either of the two horse thieves could do a thing about it, Coyote committed them all to the fight.

The moment Slocum saw Coyote reach for his gun, he focused every bit of clear thinking he had on doing the same. Fortunately, Slocum's reflexes were just sharp enough to pull the Colt from its holster and point its barrel at the three targets in front of him. Slocum knew he wouldn't be able to trust his aim as much as his draw, but he managed to pull his trigger just as Coyote cleared leather.

Brady and the kid hopped away from Coyote as the first chunk of lead ripped through the man's torso. Having drawn his own gun, Brady pointed it at Slocum and fired as quickly as he could. The kid followed suit, but was just a little slower than everyone else.

Lead hissed back and forth across the few yards or so that separated Slocum and the three gunmen. The explosion of gunfire rolled through Slocum's head as if the sounds were being filtered through water. His legs were on the verge of folding beneath him and his hands were just able to support the weight of the smoke wagon that continued to spit its fire on his behalf.

Brady was the first to stop firing, since one of Slocum's rounds caught him in the shoulder. He spun on one heel and fell sideways into the street.

Coyote staggered to the other side, where he eventually slumped against the side of a shop that was closed up for the night. He remained upright, but the wound in his chest made it difficult for him to do much more than that.

Holding his gun up to sight along its barrel, the kid fired off another round. His finger clenched around the trigger with such force that he pulled the rest of his pistol down and to the side so every one of his rounds wound up in the boardwalk. The sixth shot from Slocum's gun punched through the kid's stomach, dropping him straight down to both knees. He was still wearing his jittery expression when he collapsed.

Slocum looked around for Minh. Not only did he feel like his head was full of smoke, but his eyes were stinging from the actual smoke that now filled the air. When he found Minh, she was huddled against a locked door covering her head with both arms.

"You hurt?" Slocum asked.

She looked up and shook her head. Minh might have said something, but it was getting difficult for Slocum to hear again.

Knowing his aim had been off, Slocum examined the men in front of him. As close as they were, he should have been able to snuff them out like candles. The scene in front of him was a bloody mess. He'd fired all his shots in a rush and hit his attackers just enough to put them down. If Coyote or the other two had been smart enough to run for cover, they might have lived long enough to do some real damage.

Slocum could feel his legs starting to shake and his eyelids growing heavier. He figured there wouldn't be much time before even the wounded assholes on the ground could get the drop on him. Stepping forward slowly, Slocum emptied the bullet casings from his cylinder and reloaded the Colt. Even though the movements were second nature, he still fumbled enough to drop a few rounds onto the boardwalk before he was through.

Brady pulled himself up and then rolled onto his back. Just as he raised his gun to fire point-blank at Slocum, the rustler was cut down by a pair of shots into his chest.

Using the wall to support himself, Coyote held his breath and tightened his finger on his trigger. Slocum put one round through his forehead, which made Coyote twitch and fire his last shot into the street.

As Slocum turned to look at the last remaining gunman, he barely had enough strength to stand. When he spoke, he damn near vomited on himself. "What about you, kid?" he asked.

The kid managed to put a scowl on his face and lift his gun for one more shot. Slocum beat him to it and finished him off with a shot of his own.

Slocum began to keel over, but Minh was there to prop him up. "Where's that doctor?" he grumbled.

The doctor was only one street down from where Coyote, the kid, and Brady were lying. Minh was right when she'd told Slocum he didn't have much time to handle matters on his own. Before he even reached the doctor, he'd spat up his last few meals, and could barely keep his legs moving. Somehow, Minh helped drag Slocum to where he needed to be.

When he woke up, Slocum could see the faint rays of

dawn creeping through a nearby window. Minh stood looking down at him, and an elderly man with a wrinkled face sat on a stool next to the bed. Before Slocum could say a word, Minh held out her arms and extended every finger as if she was stretching the tendons of her hand.

"And now you see," she declared. "I bid him to rise and he rises."

The old man squinted down at Slocum and reached out to pull open his eyelids. Even though Slocum slapped his hand away, the old man clucked and shook his head solemnly. "I ain't never seen the like. He's waking up."

"Of course he wakes up," Minh said.

After looking warily at Minh, the old man leaned down until he was close enough for Slocum to smell his sour breath. "You all right, son?"

Slocum sat up and felt the room wobble a bit. Once he pulled in a few deep breaths, however, everything settled. Even his stomach had eased back down into its proper spot. "Where the hell am I?"

"I'm Doc McKay and you're in my office."

"How long have I been here?"

"This'd be the second day. This little lady brought you to me the night before last."

Slocum looked over to find Minh standing with her arms folded across her chest. She flashed him a little smirk, but put on her serious expression before Doc McKay could turn around to face her again.

"This man was sick as a dog when he came here and he was sicker the next day," McKay said to Minh. "I thought I might lose the poor soul until you came here. What the hell did you do to him?"

"I know he was sick, so I made something for him to get better," Minh replied in a thicker accent than Slocum recalled her having before.

"What did you make?"

Narrowing her eyes, Minh put an ominous tone in her voice when she told him, "Family recipe."

Judging by the look on McKay's face, he wasn't about to press her for any more than that. "Well, perhaps you can tell me about that recipe, but I should check this man out to make sure he's well enough to leave."

The doctor put Slocum through a few simple tests to make sure he could stand and walk on his own. After the old man started poking and prodding him some more, Slocum swatted the doctor's hands aside and said, "I'm fine, I'm fine. Are those my clothes?"

"Yes, but—"

"Then as soon as I'm in those clothes, I'm out that door. No more talk."

The doctor wasn't about to argue with Slocum, so he held up his hands and stepped aside.

The clothes Slocum had been wearing were neatly stacked upon a chair. Even the chain to his pocket watch was curled into an orderly pile so it didn't get tangled. His gun was in place and every bullet remaining on the gun belt was still in its loop. Now that he had his bearings as well as his things, Slocum felt a pang of guilt for barking at the old doctor that way.

"Do I owe you anything for the treatment, Doc?" Slocum asked.

The old man shook his head. "I didn't do anything more than put you in a bed. Looks like she did the real work— whatever that was."

"Well, here," Slocum said as he handed over a bit of money. "This is for the bed and your time. Thanks."

The doctor shrugged, took the money, and walked away.

Slocum followed Minh outside, where it looked to be early morning. The sun was low in the eastern sky and the air still had a cool dampness to it that went a long way in making Slocum feel more alive. Minh stood on the edge of the boardwalk, looking out at the street, and Slocum stood next to her. "What did you do to me?" he asked.

"Do?"

"Don't play dumb with me. I've still got the taste of them Chinese spices of yours in my mouth, and I know I didn't suddenly get better because of all that waving you were doing when I woke up. What did you do to me?"

Tightening a shawl around her shoulders, Minh replied, "I gave you something to make you sick. Your stomach would hurt a bit and you would pass out for a day or so."

"Hurt a bit? I puked up everything inside of me!"

Minh shrugged. "It was a powder I put on my—well, I put it on me and you ate more than I thought you would."

Slocum stared at her for a few seconds before he was able to speak. Even when he did find his words, he could scarcely believe what he was saying. "You put something on you and made me lick it off?"

"I did not make you. I did not have to make you do anything. If I remember it right, you enjoyed yourself very much."

"Yeah, I did but that's not the point. Those assholes could have killed me when I was out of sorts like that."

"Well, I didn't know they would attack you like that," Minh said. "I warned you to finish them quickly and you did. I spoke up for you when the law came by to ask what happened, and it was decided you were defending me. The sheriff was quite impressed. Or perhaps he was a marshal. He wore a badge and he was very nice. He even left you your gun."

Slocum rolled his eyes and grumbled under his breath. "So why the hell did you want to get me sick? If you wanted me to leave, you could have just asked."

"I want to stay here," she explained. "I need to make money and I can't do that by just making charms or selling spices."

"Hanging out your witch shingle, huh?"

"I thought I would try to become known as a healer. Because I'm not a doctor, I needed to show what I can do."

"So you get me sick and then miraculously heal me? There are plenty of hucksters selling tonics from wagons who use that same trick," Slocum said.

"But I am not a huckster. My medicine did work on you. I can mix plenty of other medicines for plenty of different things, but people need to see what I can do for themselves and then spread the word. Soon, some will come to me and I will help them. They will tell others, more will come, and I will be able to make a living." Seeing the stern look on Slocum's face, she added, "I will not cheat anyone."

"I'm still cross about being poisoned, is all."

Minh smiled and patted his cheek. "I could have ground it up in your coffee. I think the other way wasn't so bad."

Finally, Slocum had to admit, "I suppose it wasn't so bad at that. Will you be all right here on your own?"

"I think if any more men were coming after me, they would have done so when you were asleep. Besides, I can live here without being hunted. Folks tend to look after healers a lot more than witches. But if someone does try to harm me, I can use something I bought with Hal Singer's money." Minh hiked up her skirt just enough to show Slocum the little pistol holstered to her boot.

"The curse of flying lead." Slocum chuckled. "Works every time."

Watch for

SLOCUM AND THE BRITISH BULLY

363rd novel in the exciting SLOCUM series
from Jove

Coming in May!